THE CHRISTMAS BLANKET

A Delightful Christmas Tale

A Novella by
PHILLIP W. COOPER

COOPER DESIGN

Cooper Design

8328 S. Allegheny Avenue

Tulsa, Oklahoma, 74137

Email: coopercoolart@icloud.com

ISBN 979-8-9916130-0-2 (Paperback)

ISBN 979-8-9916130-1-9 (eBook)

To Wendell, Helen and Paul,
my loving examples of Christ.

Table of Contents

1 The Wish 3

2 The Little Boy Deep Inside. 13

3 Love Grows 23

4 The Odd Guy 27

5 Persistence of a Wish 33

6 A Life Together 41

7 The Oldest House 45

8 The Worst Day 57

9 To Much a Bother 69

10 Struggling 77

11 Total Darkness 85

12 Lifted 95

13 A Night of Jubilation 99

14 From the Mouth of Babes 103

15 Tears of Sorrow, Tears of Joy 107

16 Fear Not 115

17 My Burning Eyes 127

18 You're Crazy 131

Epilogue 135

Prologue

You never know what a child will remember. Sometimes, it's the most minor event that lodges itself into young souls. Perhaps it is God who secures particular memories so that even our adult reasoning can't shake them loose.

And if we are lucky, God will use our little memories for something extraordinary.

–Ethan Theodore Anderson

"Truly I tell you, unless you change and become
like little children, you will never enter
the kingdom of heaven."
—Matthew 18:3 (NIV)

1

The Wish

*"You'll know you're ready for the wish to come true
when you hear the angel's song."*

Grandma Ada's proclamation lured me like a big-mouth bass right into her impossible wish. My childhood imagination was saddled up and ready for the granddaddy of all wishes.

I was seven when she cast this spell upon me. No, she was not a witch, but she seemed magical with her Bible stories and lessons to be learned.

Growing up in Oklahoma, where the first hint of winter sparked everyone's holiday spirit, I would latch onto anything to do with Christmas.

"Ethan Theodore Anderson, I see you sneaking those Christmas cookies." That was the only time Mom caught me. After that, my cookie-sneaking skills became flawless. And when you add my expertise for ripping open presents, I was undoubtedly a Bona Fide Christmas Expert. One who was hopelessly chained to a glorious Christmas wish.

That wish started on one remarkable Christmas Eve. As the sun was setting, family members pulled into the gravel driveway. Car doors swung open, unleashing a whirl of cheery faces and brightly wrapped packages. There they were, aunts, uncles, and cousins, joyfully scampering through the wintry evening air into Grandma Ada and Papa Nate's cozy little house.

If you could have seen their home, you'd be convinced it had to be a worldwide sensation. Every part of the house was outlined with a gazillion multicolored lights—the big bulbs, not those little white ones. And the life-size, 60-watt plastic Santa was always there to greet us. His airbrushed, rosy cheeks and cheery smile confirmed that Christmas was at hand.

As the house churned with freshly arrived loved ones, I stood outside, mesmerized by Grandma's colorful lights. The stillness of the stars and crisp night air gently playing against my face, plus knowing that Christmas was finally here, made the night feel magical. Maybe I was an odd little kid, but something about Grandma's decorations always sparked my sense of wonder.

Suddenly the front door flew open, jarring me from my light-show trance. Cousin Rickey raced out, singing *Santa Claus Is Coming To Town.* His mouth was full of something substantial and very gooey by the looks of things.

"Ethan, guess what? Daisy got hold of Papa Nate's present and chewed it to bits."

Daisy, Grandma's Boston Terrier, found anything within her reach to be fair game.

"What'd she chew up this time?"

"Chocolates," he said, chewing and laughing. "The double-decker kind."

"Is that a piece of chocolate in your mouth?"

"Nope, it's three pieces. I bet there's still some under the tree."

Then, something caught Rickey's eye. His chewing slowed. "Hey, what's that?" he said.

I knew what he had spotted. Grandma had outdone herself by adding a new glowing wonderment, a Nativity scene. It was the one thing that could outrank even Santa on the hierarchy of Christmas spectacles. And I'll admit

I debated that fact in my young mind for a quick moment. But that night, as I beheld the beautiful manger scene with the holy incandescent Bible characters, I knew this was what Christmas was truly all about.

"Hey, there's Baby Jesus," Rickey said, captivated by the magnificent manger. He strolled closer as another chocolate mindlessly found his mouth.

We silently beheld this Heavenly grandeur, and I'm sure we looked like two additional figures in the scene. After a peaceful moment, Rickey's eyes shifted, searching for my take on Grandma's handiwork. "It's pretty cool," I assured him with a big grin.

"It's more than cool. It's cold. It's cold out here," he shouted, dashing toward the house. It was Rickey's nature to never stay in one spot for very long.

I turned back to the Nativity, sliding again into its silent embrace. I didn't notice that as Rickey ran inside, Grandma Ada came outside. It startled me when I heard her voice.

"What do you think of my new display?" she said, gathering her coat tight.

"Grandma?" I couldn't believe she was out here. Did she really leave a house full of family to come out in the cold to talk with me?

"I thought you might like it," she said.

"I love it."

One good thing about being an odd little kid and a Bona Fide Christmas Expert is that I could claim the title of *Grandchild Who Most Appreciated Grandma's Handiwork*, and I think she picked up on that.

Grandma put her arm around my shoulder, drawing me close. I sensed the importance of her giving me this moment of togetherness.

"Ethan, you really do like Christmas, don't you?"

"Yes, it's my favorite."

"Do you suppose it has something to do with that child in the manger?" she asked, guiding me closer to the scene.

"Yeah, he's the reason for the season."

"He certainly is, but there's much more to know about him. God had a wonderful plan that began with Jesus' birth. He sent his light into the world on that first Christmas night to save us from our sins. That little baby, lying in a manger, was born to die for us."

Grandma talked as though I were a grown-up, and surprisingly, I felt kind of grown-up. I understood most of what she was saying.

As we quietly admired the scene, Grandma leaned toward me and began singing her favorite Christmas song, *O Come All Ye Faithful*. Of course, the Bona Fide Christmas Expert joined in. I'll never forget our magical Christmas moment of singing to the small, glowing Jesus.

So far apart in years, yet so close in love, the two of us were feeling the specialness of God's gift to the world that night.

The chilly night air soon coaxed Grandma and me back inside, where noisy relatives were a stark contrast to the peaceful outdoors.

Aunt Lillie and Aunt Gracie were talking with Mom.

"Pardon me, pardon me," Uncle Raymond said as he masterfully slithered between the ladies, gripping a festive cup of eggnog and flashing his toothy smile.

Papa Nate unleashed more turkey aroma as he opened the oven door.

"Papa, you sure cook up a mean bird," Dad said.

"Yes, a really mean bird," Uncle Terry added.

"Don't get ahead of things. You don't know it's good till you taste it," Papa said.

My cousins, Susie and Gail, scrupulously examined Gail's plushy Christmas dress. "Mom said the lace is imported. That means it costs lots of money." Gail's superior tone always came naturally.

Then, as I suspected, Rickey and Daisy were digging for more chocolate under the Christmas tree. "Hey Ethan, I'm saving the coconut ones for you," he said.

Early on, I discovered that when my crazy relatives get together, you'll get lots of chaos: pot-stirring, loud-talking, TV-blaring, dog-barking chaos. Of course, I loved every bit of it. After all, I was a kid and a Bona Fide Christmas Expert.

As the evening progressed, we learned that Papa's turkey had indeed become a delicious, mean bird. And it didn't take long for that night's feast to transform into a messy collection of dirty plates and napkins. The men leaned back, still wrangling about sports, while the ladies took on the business of cleaning up. The cousins had settled in front of the TV to watch Rudolph and his red nose.

On my way to join the TV watchers, something caught my eye, a glimmer from Grandma's sunroom. I peered into the small chamber, where a beckoning glow from the fireplace filled the room. A silver tree lit by a softly groaning color wheel stood in the corner. It forced me to watch as it cycled through all four of its deep colors. Handmade ornaments, most of which were created by the cousins, added to the magic. I detected the familiar scent of lavender mingled with pipe tobacco.

Then I spotted an old friend, my blanket. Some folks would call it a quilt, but we always called it the Christmas Blanket.

You could find four baby blankets around Grandma's house, one for each of her grandchildren. She handmade them special by decorating for the season in which each of us was born. The Thanksgiving Blanket belonged to Gail and featured colorful leaves, Pilgrims, a turkey, and a Bible. Rickey and Susie's blankets were patriotic with stars and stripes. But my masterpiece was undoubtedly the best because it was the Christmas Blanket, and everyone knows Christmas is the most excellent holiday of all.

This blanket lured me to the loveseat, its usual resting place. Touching it, I recalled how Grandma had made it, especially for me, seven years earlier.

Running my fingers across the hand-stitching, I became mesmerized by the smoothness of the satin edges. Its sheen reflected the room's warmth. Grandma crafted doves, trees, stars, and an angel, all of which she kept beautifully simple.

The tree images and shining stars were enchanting, but my favorite was the heavenly angel, who seemed to reach out to me with good tidings.

Then, barely noticeable, I spotted Grandma's symbol, a tiny hand-stitched cross, which she placed on all of her wondrous works. This mark always excited me because it testified that this was officially one of her pieces.

"I'm gonna tell," Gail bellowed as she suddenly stood in the doorway with hands on her hips. "You're not supposed to be in here without a grown-up!"

She was reminding me about the rule made last year after Rickey used Grandma's knitting needles to roast marshmallows in her fireplace.

Gail took great delight in her tattletale skills. And enduring the Gail-scowl, I headed for the doorway. "Don't worry, I'm leaving."

I didn't mind exiting because I knew from our tradition that this room would soon host an extraordinary event, allowing my return.

Now, no matter how crazy our Christmas celebration became, Grandma Ada always made time to spend with just us kids. We were four close-in-age cousins, beginning with the likable and rambunctious Rickey. His twin sister, Susie, had curly blond hair and always giggled at my jokes. Then there was me, Ethan, the Bona Fide Christmas Expert. And finally, Cousin Gail, who always wore a fancy dress and tried to convince us she was a grown-up based solely upon her six-week age advantage.

Grandma's tradition called for the kids to break from their share of the chaos and gather in the sunroom while she read the Christmas story. We loved this part of Christmas. Even cousin Rickey managed to settle down.

Something quite magical came over Grandma as she put on her glasses and opened that colossal family Bible. The fireplace glow lit one side of her face while twinkling tree lights reflected in her glasses. Shimmering angel earrings danced playfully with each movement of Grandma's head.

I quickly secured my curl-up place next to Grandma with my special little blanket wrapped around me. Grandma had created it so Mom and Dad could bring baby me home from the hospital on that cold eighth day of December. And it didn't matter that the word "baby" was used to describe it. It belonged to me, even though, for now, it stayed with Grandma for safekeeping. Holding it tight, I listened to the soft rhythm of Grandma's reading.

Looking back, I remember something peculiar about her reading. Before the Christmas Story, she would open the enormous Bible to the page with an angel bookmark, made by the Bona Fide Christmas Expert, and read what we always called "The Blessed Rs." You know, "Blessed are the poor" and "Blessed are the meek." She would read them aloud through "Blessed are the pure in heart," but strangely, she'd stop right there every time and give me a little wink. Then, she'd turn to the book of Luke and begin the Christmas story. Every year, the same thing: pure in heart, wink, then flip over to Luke.

I never questioned this curious protocol, even though I always felt she left us and those "pure in heart" folks hanging. I hoped they'd inherit something, but before I could ponder too much, my attention would be swept away to a little town called Bethlehem.

Now, this particular Christmas Eve stood out most because it was the year Cousin Gail did the unthinkable. Just as Grandma got on a roll with Caesar Augustus and a census, Gail stopped her with an explosive question.

"Grandma, why do we always gotta read the same old story every year?"

Oh my gosh! Everyone's eyes grew wide, including Grandma's. What was Cousin Gail doing to our thing—our special Grandma thing?

An uncomfortable silence filled the room as Grandma peered at each of us over the top of her glasses. Then, I might have seen a little smile as she slowly closed her large Bible and said, "I have a splendid idea, children. Let's play a game."

"Yay," the cousins shouted.

Grandma said, "Let's play the Wish Game."

"Yippee, the Wish Game," Rickey shouted. "What's that?"

"It's simple. If you could wish for anything, and it would really, really come true, what would you wish for? Everyone is to think of just one wish."

As each of us hollered out our wishes, Grandma listened intently. She had a way of making us each feel truly special, like being the only one there in the room with her.

I can't remember specifically what any of our wishes were that night, but there was one wish I will never forget.

After much discourse about our sensational wishes and whose wish was the best, someone asked Grandma what *her* wish might be. Whoa! An abrupt silence came over the room as we tried to imagine that Grandma, of all people, could possibly have a wish of her own. And if she did, what on earth could it be?

Grandma leaned in with big eyes. "My wish?" she said, pointing to herself, "Do you really want to know? I mean, really and truly, want to know?"

"Yes, yes," the cousins answered. Even Gail was consumed with curiosity.

"Well, then I'll just tell you. Here goes."

With that, Grandma unleashed something so miraculous that its effect would remain with me for the rest of my life.

"I wish," Grandma said, "that on some special Christmas Eve, when the clock sings its midnight chimes, one of God's holy angels would appear and take my hand, leading me way back in time, more than 2,000 years, to the very night and the very place where Jesus was born."

Thoughts of angels and time travel had me spellbound.

"Oh, to see Bethlehem and the manger with all the animals. I would see Mary and Joseph, and then I would see the most beautiful infant Jesus lying there in the straw."

Right then, it occurred to me that Grandma was getting across the Christmas story despite Gail.

"And the wise men would approach riding high on their camels. Oh, how everyone would be warmed by their majestic appearance."

Had Grandma actually been there?

"Then I would look upward and see the most radiant star shining down. It would be God's way of telling us that his light had now reached into the world."

I could see a tear as Grandma told us the next part of her wish.

"I would draw close," she said, "and kneel beside the Baby Jesus and wait for Mary's nod. Then, with my softest touch, I would reach and tenderly caress the face of God. The brilliant light from the star above would reflect in his beautiful eyes, gazing up at me. Imagine that. Jesus, the Christ child, looking at me. Oh my," she sighed. "And that, my children, would be my wish."

The cousins erupted with noisy jubilation about Grandma's wish, but I was confident that my jubilation had to be the most jubilant of all.

Without thinking, I cried out, "Can I have that wish, too?"

She quickly replied, "Of course, Sweetheart, we can both have this wish."

And just like that, I had a glorious, bona fide wish destined to come true very soon.

As everyone climbed down from the loveseat, Grandma caught my attention with a rather serious look. And while the others ran ahead, she leaned close, pointing to my heart. Then, with her other hand, she pointed to her own heart and whispered, "Our wish, remember, it is our wish."

"So, we'll be there together?"

"When the wish comes true, we'll be there together," Grandma said.

Then, I asked something that surprised us both. "Can we bring my Christmas Blanket to give to Jesus?"

Grandma tilted her head. "Are you willing to give him your blanket?"

"Yeah."

She smiled and leaned close. "I tell you what. Tonight, you take the Christmas Blanket home. After all, it is your blanket, and you're now big enough to look after it. But remember, when the wish comes true, you must bring the blanket."

"Will we go tonight? It's Christmas Eve."

"Hmm," Grandma pondered. "Let's just leave that up to God and his timing. He'll know when you're ready for the wish to come true."

"But how will I know I'm ready?"

Grandma looked upward toward Heaven as if hearing God speak. Then she smiled at me and said, "One day, you'll hear an angel's song and know you're ready for the wish to come true."

And on that night, a defining wish moment was planted deep inside me.

Something in Grandma's voice that night, how she looked into our little hearts, showed me this was more than a wish. That's why I still remember that Christmas Eve night, even though time has passed and I became a grown-up.

2

The Little Boy Deep Inside

I've changed a lot since those early Christmas celebrations. At least my outward appearance has changed. But every Christmas Eve, I reconnect with the little boy deep inside and dust off the wish that belongs to Grandma and me. It's strange, but with each passing year, the wish has not faded as you might expect. Instead, it has grown stronger even though God's holy angel has not yet appeared.

So, by age 22, I had reached that milestone where a person gladly goes from student to full-blown working adult with a place of their own.

Mom and Dad helped me find an apartment. Then, they bequeathed to me the one item nobody else wanted—a massive, overstuffed chair. It's believed Uncle Terry found the behemoth at a garage sale, which sent Aunt Gracie into a tirade. Apparently, Mom and Dad acquired it to save Uncle Terry's marriage. Mom started calling it Big Chair, and that's the name that stuck. Its sole purpose was the catch-all for all sorts of clutter. "Just set that stuff on Big Chair," Mom would say.

Not far from my apartment was my new place of employment. How thrilling to have landed an accounting position with Hargrove Hospitality Solutions, a large company whose slogan is *Your Hotel Supply Leader.*

I had my own office. Tiny, but that didn't stop me from decking it out with fantastic sci-fi collectibles. I had more than enough action figures to fill my office and apartment.

After two weeks of navigating our gigantic office building, I had it all down: the parking, restrooms, and supplies. But, there was one essential room I had missed.

"Dude, you haven't tried the jelly doughnuts?" That's how Mark, the Intern, informed me about our cafeteria.

Wasting no time, I found a divine double doorway marked with the glorious word *Cafeteria*. Inside, I beheld a well-equipped food palace. Luckily, hardly anyone was there as I strolled along the food line like a general inspecting his troops.

"I'd like two jelly doughnuts, please."

The cute girl behind the counter, whose name tag read *Sonja*, said, "Fine, but you need to start at the end of the line."

I looked around, but no one was in sight. "Line?" I asked.

"Go get your tray, then come back this way."

"Will do," I said. Then, with my tray gliding along its chrome highway, I returned.

"I'm back. Did I do this right?"

"No. You need to try again."

"Um."

"Just kidding," she said.

"Okay, Sonja, do you always mess with the new guys?"

She checked her name tag. "Wait right here." She said, dashing toward a backroom. She quickly returned wearing a different name tag that read *Cindy*.

"No, Sonja, I'm not falling for your—"

"I'm Cindy. I must have grabbed the wrong tag this morning."

I gave her my best suspicious look and said, "Okay, I need two jelly doughnuts ... Sonja."

"I really am Cindy," she said, handing me my doughnuts. "So, what's your name?"

"I'm ... Leonardo," I said, keeping a straight face.

"Good to meet you, Leonardo."

"You too, Sonja."

"I'm Cindy."

"Right ... Sonja."

"It's Cindy!"

After discovering the Cafeteria, I soon became the Doughnut Master. My beltline was a testament to my frequent visits. But doughnuts were not the only thing capturing my interest.

One day, placing my order, I said, "I think I'll have just one doughnut."

"Probably a good idea," Cindy said. "Here you go, Leonardo."

"Thanks, Sonja."

As expected, she fired back, "I'm Cindy."

"Maybe I should try the sugar-free kind."

She leaned in and whispered, "Those are gross."

This felt like a good time to set things right and use her real name. "Oh, thanks, Cindy."

Her smile grew warmer as she answered, "You're welcome, Ethan."

Oh, I suspected she knew my real name, and it felt good to hear her say it.

� ☖ ☖

I liked this new, grown-up world, making friends and becoming part of the team.

We worked hard, but there were fun times, too. For example, they encouraged us to wear costumes on Halloween. I immediately thought of my favorite sci-fi movie: *Captain Hubble, Skycastor*. My limited edition Captain Hubble tee shirt, imprinted with a high-tech laser panel and cosmic ammo belt plastered across the chest, would surely be a hit.

The morning of Halloween, I Captain-Hubbled my way toward our building, practicing the notorious Hubble catchphrase where he growls, *Your time is up, my friend.*

Once inside, I immediately spotted some seriously great costumes, but I held my head high and reminded myself that nothing beats my one-of-a-kind Hubble shirt.

I headed straight to the cafeteria, hoping to impress Cindy. "No way!" I couldn't believe my eyes. Cindy had on my exact same shirt. How could she have the ultra-rare Captain Hubble shirt? What are the odds?

I marched right up to her. "Hey."

She smiled as she noticed my shirt. "Is there a problem?"

Pointing at our shirts, "There can't be two Captain Hubbles."

She giggled as she took my hand. "Sure, there can. If we stand close together—like this—we can be Captain Double."

I tried to remain serious but couldn't hide my laughter. "Captain Double. That's a good one."

We stood side by side, and suddenly, words jumped out of my mouth. "We should find a party tonight and go together as Captain Double."

Cindy smiled. "Some of us are going to Willow Ranch for a huge costume party tonight. We should go?"

"I'm available," I said.

"Okay, Captain Double, it is," she said, laughing.

Feeling good, I growled the Hubble catchphrase.

Cindy looked horrified. "You should never do that again," she said, and by the looks of nearby coworkers, I knew she was right. But I felt proud of myself for finally asking Cindy out. Or did she ask me?

That night, the old barn at Willow Ranch had become the very definition of Halloween. Hundreds of pumpkins lined the path to the spooky barn. Spooky because purple lights painted it with an eerie glow. Leaves swirled around the twin Captains as we headed to the barn.

The party greeted us with an army of bloody faces, glow-in-the-dark jewelry, and fake-leather Gothic madness, all rocking to the *Ghost Busters* theme song.

"Look at those costumes."

"Hey, Captain Double has arrived," she said. "Let's have some fun."

She grabbed my hand, and we danced our way into the mob. Cindy stared at me. "Awesome," she said, pointing at me.

"Thanks. You're an awesome dancer, too."

"Not that. Look at our shirts."

Wow, our Captain Hubble T-shirts glowed in the dark. Radiant orange control panels and green ammo belts made us look spectacular.

So, the two glowing Captains danced, snacked, and chatted with friends, making this the best party ever, all because of Cindy. As the hours passed, the music suddenly stopped, and an announcer blared, "It's Costume Showcase time. Who will win one of our extravagant trophies? Line up, and everyone gets a turn to show their stuff."

The music roared back, and we secured our place in line. The spotlight revealed lots of vampires and zombies, but, thankfully, no Captain Hubbles.

When our turn came, I twirled Cindy into the spotlight, showing off our Hubble fashions. Then Cindy yelled to the crowd, "We're Captain Double!" She held up two fingers. "Get it? ... Double instead of Hubble?"

Her explanation garnered a few laughs, but the surprising part—get this—when they handed out awards, our costume came in third. We couldn't stop laughing when they presented our cheesy trophy. It featured a small plastic bat glued to an empty toilet paper roll where green glitter letters spelled out, *3rd Place, Worst Costume.* And I'm still unsure if that was better or worse than 1st Place Worst Costume. Nonetheless, Cindy and I loved it.

After receiving our lovely award, a wicked witch ran up to us. "Hello, Ethan. Nice trophy"

I must have looked confused.

"You doofus. It's me, your cousin Gail."

"Gail, your face! It's so green. Aren't you supposed to be in Chicago?"

"I come back every Halloween to meet up with my high school buddies."

I looked around. "Buddies?"

"Well, that's the thing. Apparently, they're all married, having babies, and drifting away. Looks like I'm the last holdout."

"You party animal."

Gail rolled her eyes. "Listen, can I hang out with you guys for a while? This witch is in no condition to fly back home."

I glanced at Cindy, her eyebrows raised. "Oh, Cindy, this is my cousin Gail. And this is Cindy."

Cindy offered her hand. "Please join us."

Just then, Aladdin, who closely resembled Mark, the intern, walked by shouting, "Hey, Captain Double, congrats on your trophy."

Cindy waved our spectacular toilet paper roll and hollered, "Woohoo. Thanks, Mark. I mean Aladdin."

I was about to growl my Hubble catchphrase, but Cindy gave me a don't-you-dare look.

It was good that we found Gail. She needed some company, and Cindy seemed eager to meet one of my relatives and dig into my past.

As the party wound down, we headed to Kate's Diner to keep the fun going. Walking in, I saw King Arthur with a zombie cheerleader and felt relieved we weren't the only costumed customers.

Finding a booth, Cindy immediately started in. "Okay, Gail, spill all your good stories about Ethan growing up."

"Ooh, let's see. It was Grandma's house, where we spent most of our time together."

I chimed in. "That's Grandma Ada. She's the one who made us all really cool baby blankets,"

Gail turned to me. "Do you still have the Christmas Blanket?"

"Forever and ever," I said.

"I'm not surprised. Ethan was always so into Christmas, and Grandma would egg him on."

"Hey, we all loved Christmas."

"Yeah, but you and Grandma were always dreaming up stuff. Like that ridiculous wish thing. You were so goofy, the way you went on about the angel coming with a time machine and hauling you guys off to see Jesus."

"It was Grandma's wish game. You loved it, too."

"But you two were really going to fly off, time traveling to the Holy Land." Gail turned to Cindy. "Supposedly, an angel will come someday and take Ethan and Grandma Ada back in time to see the Nativity.

"It wasn't like that." I tried to soften Gail's words.

"And it had to be midnight on Christmas Eve to work. I can't believe Grandma Ada encouraged such craziness."

I glanced at Cindy, trying to read her reaction. Then I said, "Well, we had fun. Grandma loves to bring joy to her grandkids."

"She loved to mess with us. Grandma thinks kids need lots of magic for some reason."

Gail was at it again. Why did I invite her?

Cindy finally spoke up. "She sounds fascinating."

I kept trying to cushion this conversation. "Gail, you loved —"

"No! You totally bought into all her crap. But hey, we're grown-ups now, right? Can't you see how she filled our little heads with malarkey? Oh, and get this, she read to us from her huge Bible with that Old English jargon. I never could get into that."

I wanted to scream at Gail to stop. "Well, I loved Grandma's malarkey.

"I guess we're not totally messed-up adults," Gail said. "We do have a grip on reality, right?"

Cindy must have wanted to change the subject as much as I did. "So, what do you know about Ethan's first girlfriend?"

"Oh. That would be Bobbi Sue Walker back in Sunday school."

"Don't go there," I said.

"She had massive hair and those big black socks that never stayed up."

"No. No. You're thinking of Valerie."

"It was Bobbi Sue. You carved her name on your baseball bat.

"Wow, Cousin, you sure have a good memory. You can stop now."

Cindy laughed at our weird conversation. I hoped she was taking it lightly.

Later, as I drove Cindy home, I steered our conversation away from Gail's poisonous comments. "What a great party," I said. "But we should have worked up a cool dance to better sell the Captain Double concept."

"What? And mess up our chances for winning this?" She said, holding our loser trophy.

"But imagine us doing a cool Captain Double dance, and suddenly, everyone backs up, forming a circle, cheering our dazzling choreography.

You know, like in the movies."

"Ethan, you are an odd guy, aren't you?"

She was right. I always knew I had an odd side. As I already mentioned, I was an odd little kid. And apparently, I had become an odd, big kid who clings to fantasies easier than most.

3

Love Grows

This new grown-up life was fantastic. I had a fun job, a cheap apartment, and a beautiful girlfriend who seemed okay with my oddness.

We spent fall weekends at every small-town festival we could find. Pumpkin bread and caramel corn went straight to my waistline. Cindy was so much fun, and we quickly became an item. Of course, when the offer came, I jumped at having Thanksgiving dinner with Cindy and her family. But when Thanksgiving finally arrived, all I could think was, what if her folks hate me? What if I say something wrong?

It was Thanksgiving day, and standing on her front porch, I took a deep breath to stay calm. My hand shook as I reached for the doorbell—DING-DONG. Cindy's dad, Stan, yanked open the door. His serious expression probed deep into my eyes. Yikes, what had I gotten myself into? Then he asked the strangest question. "What do frogs like to drink?"

I panicked. Was this a secret code? A password to gain entrance?

He grew a big smile. "Croak-A-Cola," he said, reaching for a handshake.

We both laughed, but mine was nervous laughter as he led me to the kitchen. Cindy, her mom, Gloria, and two sisters, Brook and Avery, were cooking up a storm, and the wonderful aroma confirmed their culinary expertise. It's a wonder her dad didn't weigh 600 pounds.

The four amazing chefs were thrilled to see me and were not shy about hugging. Cindy's mom handed me a stack of napkins and said, "Here ya go. Set one to the right of each plate."

It surprised me how quickly I became part of the family.

As we settled around the lavishly set table, a knock interrupted, and a young man entered. "Hi, just me," he said.

"Get in here, Danny," Stan said.

A smiling young man entered, holding a brown paper bag tied with a red bow and the word *Pecans* handwritten on the side.

"Mom wants you to have these for helping us with meals."

"Tell her thanks," Gloria said. "You know we always love to cook."

"Danny, this is Ethan," Stan said.

I stood and shook his firm grip. "Don't get up," he said. "I'm just here for a minute."

As Stan built a heaping plate for Danny, he asked, "What do you call a turkey that's running?"

Danny smiled at us and shrugged.

"Fast food," Stan said.

We all laughed, and Cindy rolled her eyes.

Danny sniffed the plate as he headed toward the door. "Smells mighty good. I hate to impose on you, nice folks."

Cindy handed him a bag of extra rolls. "You're not imposing. Tell Louise happy Thanksgiving."

"You guys are the best," he said as he dashed away.

I had to agree with Danny's statement.

After a sumptuous dinner, everyone stacked their plates in the sink and headed for the living room.

"Dad will do the dishes later. That's how things work around here," Cindy said.

"It's a good trade-off," Stan said.

The Turner family was a loving bunch, sharing delightful stories that enticed me into overstaying my welcome. I finally donned my jacket and bid everyone a Happy Thanksgiving. That's when Stan handed me a Christmas present. "Before you go, you're going to need one of these for Christmas. Go ahead, open it."

I peeled away the wrapping and examined a box that read, *Dog Choir Doorbell. Enjoy Dogs barking your favorite Christmas tunes every time visitors arrive.*

Stan's eyes lit up. "It has *Deck the Halls* and *Jingle Bells*. You'll love it."

"This looks so cool. I can't wait to try it. Thanks, Mr. Turner."

Cindy and I walked to my car. "I need to buy your dad a present."

"Oh, gosh, don't worry about it. He bought a case of those crazy doorbells, and he's handing them out like candy."

Cindy and I were growing close. I could be my odd self around her. We shared our thoughts on everything. However, the topic of religion made us feel a little awkward.

"When I was little," Cindy said, "our family attended several churches. Baptists, Methodists, it didn't seem to matter. Then, Mom and Dad found a small church in Arlinville. That's where we met Danny and his mom, Louise. The church was large at one time, and Pastor Peterson nurtured hundreds of members. But as the town dwindled, the church finally had to close. A remnant of worshipers now meet at the Pastor's house, which feels more like family. My favorite thing about this church is the midnight Christmas service. The candles and music are so amazing."

Cindy painted her Christianity with a loving brush. But reaching for my paintbrush, I realized my Christian journey had slipped a few notches. Did that odd little Christmas expert who loves Jesus become a lazy Christian? My church attendance had suffered under the pretense of being busy. Yet it's strange how I've clung fervently to an outlandish belief that a time travel wish will indeed carry Grandma and me to the first Noel to see the Baby Jesus. How could I word it so Cindy would not think I was completely crazy? Or, as she's already said, *odd*.

I had to tell her something, so I started by saying, "I grew up attending a small church with many of my family members. Grandma Ada and Papa Nate, bless his soul, were the greatest examples of Christianity. As Gail said, Grandma always read the Bible and taught us about Jesus. She could take anything and turn it into a lesson about God's love. There are a lot of Biblical seeds planted inside me. I have no gold stars for church attendance, especially these days. But thanks to Grandma Ada, I embrace a strong connection to Jesus."

I needed to tell her I believed in the wish, so I continued, "Grandma told us kids about her wish to travel back in time to see the first Noel. I know it sounds weird, right?"

"It sounds sweet," Cindy said.

I froze and couldn't find the words. I would need more time to think this through.

4

The Odd Guy

As Christmas neared, I decided it was time to introduce Cindy to Mom and Dad. They were ready to meet the one I'd been gushing about. Dinner on Christmas Eve would be the perfect occasion. But first, there was one thing I had to do. Cindy needed to know about my faith in the outlandish wish. So, how do I keep from sounding completely insane? Maybe if I tell her, there's still a little boy inside me who believes in an impossible wish. Or, what if I show her the Christmas Blanket? She would surely see the joy of the wish. I knew it was risky, but I needed to be honest. So, I called her.

"Cindy, what are you doing right now? Cause, I'd love for you to come see my place.

"Oh. I suppose I can break from doing my sock drawer. Shall I bring anything?"

"Nope. Just come over."

Even though my apartment was cramped, I was still excited to show her my excellent sci-fi touches.

Before Cindy could knock at my door, I swung it open. "There you are."

Cindy entered, scanning the room like a kid at an amusement park. "Wow! Look at this. And I thought your office had a lot of action figures.

"My favorites stay here so I can keep an eye on them."

"Did it take long to collect all these?"

"Let's just say there are a lot of flea markets that know me by name."

Her jaw dropped, and she zoomed over to my favorite Captain Hubble action figure. "Look at that," she said. "Pretty awesome."

"Oh! wait a minute." I scrounged through my dresser, pulled out our lovely Third Place trophy, and placed it next to Captain Hubble. "That's better."

Then, Cindy spotted another Hubble figure and carefully placed it so two Hubbles were next to the trophy. "There. Perfecto."

I smiled at Cindy. "I'm dying to growl the Hubble catchphrase right now."

"No!" she said.

"I can't help it."

"Don't do it," she warned.

"Here it comes."

"No. You're just going to embarrass yourself."

I put my arms around her. "Here, it comes."

She twisted away, laughing, and covered her ears. "Fine, just get it over with."

I paused for a second, then said, "I think I'll save it for later."

"Hurry, get it over with."

"Oh, now you *want* me to do the phrase?" I said, embracing her again.

"No. I want ... I want—" Cindy suddenly pressed her lips against mine. Was I dreaming? She held me close. I pulled her even closer. I could feel her warmth through her soft sweater. Everything was swirling, and Cindy and I were soaring together for that instant.

I had not experienced many kisses, but this one ranked the highest—the kind that changes a person.

She leaned back a little, staring at my lips. "Ethan, I—" Suddenly, we kissed again. Then she stepped away, looking at the ceiling and breathing deeply. "I don't know what to say." Then, to dissuade awkwardness, she asked, "Do you have a Coke or something?"

"Pepsi?"

"That would be awesome."

After that unbelievable kiss, I hoped the wish might sound less crazy.

Handing her a Pepsi, I said, "Here, have a seat in Big Chair."

She sat, noticing the chair's exceptional comfort. "Oh. I might just fall asleep in this thing."

"That's his name, you know."

"What name?"

"Big Chair. That's what we've always called him."

"Hello, Big Chair. So nice to meet you," she said, petting it like a dog.

"Oh, he likes that."

Cindy stared at me. "Yep, I was right. You are an odd guy."

"What? Doesn't everybody have 400 amazing action figures and a ridiculously humongous chair?"

Cindy leaned back laughing, causing the Christmas Blanket to slide around her shoulders. She lifted it for a closer look. "Wow. What a beautiful little quilt."

"Remember? I mentioned Grandma Ada and her blankets. This is the one she made for me."

"Grandma Ada does amazing work."

It sounded good to hear Cindy mention Grandma's name. "Grandma still tries, but her hands give her trouble these days."

"Will I get to meet her on Christmas Eve?"

"Yes, she's eager to meet you. Her memory gets a little fuzzy since Papa Nate passed away."

Cindy looked again at the blanket. "It's a Christmas Blanket."

"I was born in December, so, she made my blanket Christmassy."

"Yeah, makes sense."

Was this the time to bring up the wish? I had to try. "Cindy." She looked at me with warm eyes. "About the blanket."

"Yes?"

"As long as I can remember, I have had that blanket. There's something about Grandma Ada and that blanket."

"Yeah?"

"It's special, or maybe 'magical' is a better word."

"Magical?"

"As a child, I absolutely loved Christmas at Grandma's house. There was one Christmas Eve when something happened, and Cousin Gail mentioned some of it on Halloween. Grandma invented a game where each of us revealed a wish. We called it the Wish Game and conjured up all sorts of wild wishes. Then Grandma revealed her wish to go back in time to see the first Noel."

"Oh yes, the Nativity thing your cousin talked about?"

"Yeah, but not entirely like what she said. Grandma wished to witness the baby Jesus and the first Christmas as it actually happened—the real Nativity."

"That's such a beautiful thought," Cindy said.

"Well, there's more. I kinda latched onto Grandma's wish. And she and I agreed that when God allows the wish to happen, we will meet back in time together."

"That's darling. I can see little Ethan, who is all excited to travel in time," Cindy said.

"Well, how about big Ethan?"

Cindy looked confused. "What about him?"

I sighed and looked away. "You know how you say I'm an odd guy?" I looked back at Cindy, "Well, you're right because I still believe that crazy wish will come true."

Cindy tried to process my story. "Is it one of those, wouldn't-it-be-nice kind of wishes? Or is it the kind where you seriously expect this to happen?"

I sat there searching for an answer.

"So it's not a sweet thing, but more of a weird thing?" she asked.

"No. Well, it's a little weird, but it's sweet too. It's hard to explain how the wish and the little boy inside me conspire, making me cling to something impossible. It's like miracles in the Bible. Do you believe God parted the Red Sea? Or turned water into wine?"

"I do believe the Bible."

"Well, it's kind of the same. Bible miracles happened long ago, but I believe God has 'miracles' yet to come. That's what this would be, a future miracle."

I couldn't think of any other way to say it. "Cindy, Someday I will be at the actual Nativity of Jesus. Or, you could say I was actually there. Except I haven't gone yet." The more I tried to explain, the more ridiculous it sounded.

Cindy seemed troubled. "You honestly believe that you and your grandmother are going to time travel 2,000 years and see the infant Jesus?"

"Um, something like that?" This was quickly going downhill.

Cindy stood, shaking her head and grabbing her coat. "That's pretty odd, all right." Then, with confusion in her voice, she said, "I should go."

The voice in my head was screaming, "No! Don't go." But those words would not come out. I had botched a great evening. I was falling in love with Cindy and wanted to be completely honest with her, even when it seemed so crazy. Why did I risk losing her forever? If only I could turn back the clock for a do-over.

After that blunderous night, Cindy disappeared. My calls went unanswered. At work, she stayed out of sight. I knew I had lost her. With our Christmas Eve dinner only a week away, it became clear that Cindy would not be there.

I was drowning in misery and ready to give up. A few days later, after work, while walking to my car, I found a note on my windshield which read, *Dear Odd Guy, turn around and look.*

I turned to see Cindy walking toward me. "Ethan, I got all your messages. I just needed some time."

"I know I sounded crazy. I'm so sorry."

"Don't be sorry," she said. "Believe it or not, I've missed you. I've missed your oddness. It makes no sense, but oddness seems to be something I like about you."

"Really? That's the greatest thing I could ever hear."

Cindy took my hands and said, "I can see your passion and hope. I get it now." Then she gave me something I thought would never again happen: a warm loving hug.

Cindy was still interested in me—in us. I knew I needed to tone down the wish stuff. But at least she realized how important the wish was to me.

5

Persistence of a Wish

When Christmas Eve finally arrived, dinner smelled delicious, and the house oozed with cozy holiday decor.

I wore my ugly sweater—odd guy worthy. Mom and Dad were excited to meet my perfect human being. Grandma Ada looked fabulous, wearing her angel earrings, as I requested. Dad kept checking his watch. All we needed was Cindy.

Finally, we heard the Dog Choir doorbell. I bounced to my feet with a huge smile and opened the door. My huge smile faded as I tried to understand what I was seeing. There stood Cindy, wearing handcuffs. And next to her, a police officer. It was awkward as we stood there looking at each other while electronic dogs barked out Jingle Bells.

The policeman had to yell over the holiday barking, "I hate to bother you, folks. I found this young lady snooping around your windows."

"I wasn't snooping," Cindy hollered.

"We've had reports—" the dog choir finished, and the officer resumed in a normal tone "—reports of burglaries in this area. She claims she's a guest of yours."

"This is all so weird," I said.

"So you can vouch for her?"

"Hmm–"

"Ethan. Don't you dare," Cindy said.

"Yes, officer, we've been expecting her."

The officer swiftly removed the handcuffs. "Sorry for the inconvenience, Ma'am. You folks have a merry Christmas."

Once inside, Cindy looked highly embarrassed. Rubbing her freshly released wrists, she said, "I'm so sorry for my dreadful grand entrance. I really do have a good excuse." Cindy glanced at me and continued. "The wind is so strong tonight, and my scarf took flight when I stepped out of the car. I think it landed in your bushes."

"Yes, it's been gusty all day," Dad said.

"I looked around your bushes, and who knew the police were so diligent?"

"It's okay, Honey," Mom said.

Eager to move the topic onto a positive note, I held up a finger to get everyone's attention. "Grandma, Mom, Dad, I present Cindy Turner."

Dad stood and said, "It's great to finally meet you, Cindy."

Mom reached for Cindy's hands and said, "I bet we can find your scarf."

"Well, it might be in the next county," Cindy said.

I again held up a finger. "Grandma Ada, this is Cindy."

"How nice you could be with us, sweetheart."

I could see Cindy's genuine excitement about meeting my fellow time traveler. "I've heard so many great things about you, Grandma Ada. Ethan showed me one of your amazing creations, his Christmas blanket."

"Oh yes, I just loved making that one."

Cindy's eyes grew wide, and she dashed out the door, leaving us to wonder. A moment later, she returned with a covered dish. "I took the liberty of bringing a broccoli casserole. We Turner girls hate to show up empty-handed."

Mom took the dish. "That smells delicious. I'm so glad you brought this." Then Mom whispered to Cindy, "I worried about having made enough food. This will be perfect."

As we gathered around the table, compliments were plentiful. I was thrilled to see a natural attraction between Cindy and Grandma. "Cindy, have you ever tried your hand at quilting?" Grandma asked.

"I'm afraid sewing is way beyond me."

"Oh, it might be easier than you think." Grandma pulled from her purse a small package wrapped in tissue. "I want you to have this."

A look of wonder came over Cindy as she carefully unwrapped a small plush lamb, hand-sewn with perfect craftsmanship. "It's not a quilt but uses the same skills as quilting.

"I love this," Cindy said.

"I made this one as a child's toy, but you can make them as tree ornaments or even a dog toy if you add a squeaker. You must let me show you how to make them."

"Wait, let me see that," I said, examining it closely. "Yep. There it is—Grandma's sign." I held it where Cindy could see the little cross stitched in.

"Oh," she said. "It's like the one on your Christmas Blanket." Cindy caressed the lamb with her cheek. "I would love to learn how to make something so precious."

"I think I can work you into my busy schedule," Grandma chuckled.

As Cindy carefully re-wrapped the lamb, Dad stood, holding a small gift bag. "Since it seems to be time for gifts."

"Uh oh. Is that what I think it is?" I said.

"Now, wait a minute. You don't know for sure."

"Let me guess. It's the same thing you got me last year, right?"

"Why do you think that?"

"Because you give me the same thing every year."

"Well, it appears we have a tradition here. Do you want it or not?"

I fished out my car keys and demonstrated a dim little flashlight. "I definitely need a new one."

Dad smiled as he tossed me the sack. "Here. Merry Christmas." Soon, I was dazzling everyone with my bright new keychain flashlight. "Thanks, Dad. I love our tradition."

Our fun evening seemed to fly by. Not even Cindy's startling entrance had dampened this party.

Cindy obviously enjoyed meeting the folks. But not wanting to wear out her welcome, she stood and bid everyone goodbye. As I escorted her outside, I proudly lit the front yard with my keychain flashlight. Cindy suddenly took off running, "There you are," she yelled, displaying her wayward scarf like a trophy.

I laughed. "Oh, so there really *is* a scarf."

"Stop it, Ethan. You've seen me wear this."

I opened her car door. "Good night, Ethan. I had the best time. Your folks are amazing." Then she kissed me, and I again felt transported into bliss.

As I strolled back inside, Dad said, "That's a wonderful girl you've found."

"She's a cutie," Mom added.

I smiled. "I'm so glad you like her." Then I noticed Grandma frowning and giving a thumbs down.

"What?" I said.

She began laughing as she changed to a thumbs-up.

"Grandma, you had me worried."

"Don't worry; we know a good person when we see one." Then Grandma lifted her help-me-up arm. "I'm ready to go home now. Ethan, would you be so kind?"

"Of course, I'll drive you. I don't want you getting run over by a reindeer."

She shook her fist. "I'm not afraid of old Rudolph."

Grandma seemed extra feisty that night. Perhaps there was something in her eggnog. Then, heading out the door, she mischievously pressed the barking doorbell. We could hear laughter from inside.

Grandma was always fun, and now that I'm older, she shows more of her zany side.

As we drove, Grandma asked about the Christmas Blanket. "It's right here, in my duffel bag."

"Wonderful," Grandma said. "Tonight is Christmas Eve, a grand night for a wish to come true."

"You think it will happen tonight?"

Grandma peered at me. "Don't you believe?"

"I do believe. You told me I'd be ready someday."

"Maybe we're ready tonight," Grandma said.

I felt encouraged. In all my years of waiting for the wish, I had never shared the vigil with Grandma. It never seemed necessary, but maybe that's what has been missing.

"Grandma, I've been wondering; have you already been to the Nativity?"

"Been there? I doubt God would bless only me when it's *our* wish."

"I know, but sometimes you describe the wish like you were there."

"Oh, that," she said, "That's the Holy Spirit. When we make Jesus our Lord, the Spirit dwells in us and councils us. So, he has shown me glimpses of Jesus' birth in my spirit." She turned, looking at me. "Are there times when you just seem to know something?"

"I have heard a voice that comes from deep inside. Not a real voice."

"That's how it works. It's a quiet voice," she said.

"So those glimpses, is that how the wish will come true, instead of actually being there?"

Grandma looked puzzled. "Is that your wish? A vague glimpse of the Nativity? Or do you really and truly want to be there, feel the night breeze, smell the animals in the stable, and see the glorious light from his star?"

"All these years, I've dreamed of really being there," I said.

"Ethan, there's no miracle too big for God. My wish is to see and feel everything about Bethlehem and know I am actually standing there."

"I want that, too."

For some time, I had carried a nagging thought concerning the wish, so I had to ask, "Grandma, does the wish seem selfish sometimes? Like we're just indulging ourselves?"

She took off her glasses, and as she cleaned them, she asked, "Was the blind man, whom Jesus healed, selfish because he wanted his sight?

"But that seems different?"

"Listen, we can't see the world 2,000 years ago. We can't see baby Jesus." Then, putting her glasses back on, she said, "But like the blind man, we want to see. We hope to see. The 15th chapter of Romans says *God is the God of hope, so we may abound in hope.* The wish is all about hope."

As I mulled over her encouraging words, she continued. "Ethan, let me tell you a story. Mamma and Daddy took me to a parade when I was a little girl. Lots of people lined the street. I mean a lot of people. Then, as the parade marched along, I tried desperately to see. I could hear horses clomping and the sounds of a marching band, but they were only glimpses. I was in a canyon of tall grown-ups and wished so hard to see. Then Daddy smiled at me and lifted me up. Suddenly, I could see it all. The glorious bits and pieces came into focus as I witnessed the marvelous parade firsthand. It took a father's love to lift me up where I could see."

I never thought of it like that, but Grandma's words lifted me. I regained my trust in the wish.

Just minutes before midnight, we arrived at Grandma's house. I was pleased to see Plastic Santa. His paint had faded, but his smile was still jovial. And the glowing Nativity seemed smaller, but it still sparked my sense of wonder.

We hurried inside, and not surprisingly, Grandma immediately began making hot chocolate. I extracted the Christmas Blanket and draped it across Grandma's chair. With just minutes to go, we sat quietly, waiting for the clock to herald the coming miracle.

It felt good to be with Grandma, sharing our wishful vigil. I sipped my hot chocolate and noticed Grandma's demeanor. Before tonight, I wondered if she had been humoring me all these years, or was she truly instilled—like me—with the excitement of the wish? But I could see the signs: the way she kept looking at the clock, her quiet breathing, and her ears anticipating any little sound. I was well acquainted with all these signs.

Sitting quietly, we heard the click of clock hammers rearing back, then "BONG." The chimes began their 12-note song, filling the room with high expectations. I nervously adjusted my chair, which brought Grandma's shushing finger to her lips. As the last chime faded, we waited.

Then, near the ceiling, a light appeared. It trailed slowly across the wall but quickly revealed itself as headlights from a passing car. We sighed and resumed our anticipation. After a long, high-alert moment, we realized this year would be like all the others. Our angel would be a no-show.

Then Grandma's eyes widened as she pointed toward the window. I turned and saw movement on the porch.

"Someone's out there," she whispered.

I quietly peeked out the door. I couldn't believe it; a mysterious figure was moving toward me.

The motion-sensor porch light kicked on, and we heard, "Ho, ho, ho, Merry Christmas."

I turned to Grandma. "It's Santa?"

His enormous eye surveyed through the door crevice. "Have you been good little boys and girls?"

"You've got the wrong house," Grandma hollered.

I opened the door wide, revealing a confused Santa. Then, he used his non-Santa voice. "Is this the Boyer's house?"

"No, Honey, they're the next street over."

"Oops, sorry." Santa quickly turned to leave and gave out one last Santa voice. "Merry Christmas."

I closed the door and glanced at Grandma. "Well, not exactly an angel."

Grandma chuckled, saying, "Yeah, but he is a saint."

We laughed as we lifted our hot chocolates. "To Saint Nicholas," I said.

"Here, here," Grandma said, taking a sip.

6

A Life Together

Entering a new year, Cindy and I became ever closer. My hopes grew that she would someday become my wife. From the lilt in her voice and how she smiled, I suspected she had similar hopes.

I tried to recall the style of jewelry Cindy liked. Apparently, I'm not very observant. So, one day, while we enjoyed an afternoon at Walnut Park, I found myself staring at her earrings.

"What are you looking at?" she said.

"Just figuring out your taste in jewelry."

"Really? All this time, and you've never noticed?"

"Just wanting to make sure," I said, shifting my gaze to her necklace.

"Okay, Odd Guy, what's this about?"

"I'm terrible at this."

"At what?"

I gave up any attempt to be subtle and came right out and said, "Cindy, I think we should go look at rings."

"What?" she said, trying to hold back a smile. "Is there something you want to ask me?"

"Well. Cindy." She tilted her head, expecting something profound. I knew

I would blow it no matter what, so I just came out with it. "It's just that some-day, when I get on one knee and you open that little velvet box, I want it to be perfect. Exactly the ring that you'll love forever."

"Oh, Ethan," she said, hugging me. "You're just so different from anyone I've ever met."

"Cindy, I love you. I think you should be my wife."

She stared at me with huge eyes. I thought I had blown it until she said, "I love you so much, Ethan. I've dreamed of becoming your wife. Yes. Yes. I accept your proposal."

Proposal? I just proposed? Imagine that.

Our smiles and embrace said it all. Then I chuckled, saying, "This is not how I pictured it would happen."

"It's beautiful, as only an odd guy could do. I wouldn't want it any other way." And then came another glorious kiss.

Wedding plans were set in motion. We found that perfect ring, the one she would love forever. And I did get down on one knee for a proper proposal. We settled on the 5th day of August for no particular reason other than it fit family schedules.

The world's cheapest wedding is how we would look back on our special day. It didn't matter that Cindy wore her sister's wedding gown. Or that her cafeteria coworkers provided the catering. And my one and only suit served quite well, although I splurged on a new tie. Plus, the flowers harvested from Mom's gardens looked terrific.

Our families and many friends filled the little church of my youth. Seeing so many smiling faces felt encouraging, but when Cindy walked down the aisle, her smile lit the chapel like the noon sun on a cloudless day.

No one would ever suspect our meager price tag for such a splendid affair. And by the end of the day, Mr. and Mrs. Anderson were headed to the Ozark

Mountains for a fantastic honeymoon. Fantastic, despite our lack of motel reservations during fishing season.

✄ ✄ ✄

It was an exceptional day as we stepped into our newlywed life. Boxes of Cindy's things were stacked in the middle of my small apartment—or, should I say, *our* apartment. My action figure museum would have to scale back, and before Cindy could say anything, I blurted, "One shelf. I can fit all the sci-fi stuff on one shelf."

She gave me a look and reached into a box, extracting a rolling pin, which made me a little nervous. "Three," she said. "You need at least three shelves."

She then turned toward the kitchen, opened all the cabinets, and gazed at the considerable lack of kitchen items. She waved her rolling pin like a pointer, calculating to herself. "Okay, it will be tight, but I think all my kitchen things will fit."

Next, we examined the tiny bathroom. "Only one sink?" Cindy asked.

"We could take turns?"

She smiled. "Relax, I grew up with two sisters; I'm good at sharing." Then she planted a little kiss on my cheek.

We explored our marital roles. "I'll be the chef," Cindy said.

"And I can dust the action figures." Immediately, I realized my lame humor, and I quickly backtracked. "I mean, do the dishes." Cindy flashed me a stern look, followed by a tiny chuckle.

This new, fun journey was like playing house.

The next day, the doorbell rang. "Our first visitor," Cindy said, opening the door. Grandma Ada stood there with a big smile. I could see she was up to something, especially when Dad walked in with two boxes.

"I just couldn't wait to come visit," Grandma said with big hugs for us.

Dad laid down the boxes and said, "Sorry, guys. I told her to call first."

"I wanted to surprise you. Cindy, I hope you don't mind, I brought you some things you'll need as I teach you how to quilt." She handed Cindy a basket. "Here is your very own sewing kit. It's not a wedding gift. This is just for you."

Cindy opened the basket like a child on Christmas morning. "I love this," she said, lifting out pinking shears.

"And here's a box of quilt scraps for practice. Once you've settled in, we'll begin lessons."

"How about right now?" Cindy said.

Grandma smiled. "I was hoping you'd say that."

Grandma and Cindy dove into the sewing kit goodies and the assortment of fabrics. Then, in a very short time, Cindy displayed an Ada-style dove image saying, "Look what I made."

"That's awesome," I said. "It looks very familiar."

"I hope so. I tried to match the one on your Christmas blanket."

"You're making your own Christmas blanket?"

Cindy rolled her eyes. "There's only one Christmas blanket, my dear."

7

The Oldest House

Even our cramped apartment could not hinder the joy of our early years. And by our fifth anniversary, we had reached a slightly more mature level in life. I became the Assistant Accounting Manager, which meant a bigger office and a smaller sci-fi collection. And not surprisingly, Cindy found a great job involving food. An up-and-coming pizza franchise discovered her superb kitchen and office skills. Life at the Andersons was running smoothly.

We both felt it was time to grow our family. Every time we discussed having kids, our tight apartment always chimed in. We needed a bigger place in a good area. It was fun as we searched every part of town, but we quickly realized our dream did not align with our price range.

"This is harder than I thought," Cindy said.

"Maybe we're being too picky."

Cindy took my hand and said, "Let's try something—a prayer."

We sat on the edge of our bed as Cindy began, "Father in Heaven, you are nudging us toward a new home. Please lead us to the place you would have us be. A place with good neighbors and large enough to raise children. A home where we will always honor you as Lord. May it be where your love flows freely, and your holy angels are always welcome. Guide us to that special home that you have for us. In the name of Jesus, amen."

Then Cindy gave me a smile and said, "I added that holy angel part just for you."

"Yes, I caught that, thanks."

"Ethan, if you could live anywhere regardless of the price, where would you want to live?"

I didn't hesitate, "Walnut Street."

"Me too," Cindy said. "Those vintage houses are like going back in time."

"There's no way we could afford to live there. It would take a miracle."

The following Sunday at church, our real estate friend Deborah ran up to us very excited. "It needs some love," she said, handing us a sheet of paper. "But it has lots of potential."

"Deborah, you know, we've looked all over—"

"They just lowered the price for a second time. It's worth a look."

"Okay, where is this place?" Cindy asked.

"Walnut Street."

Cindy and I stared at each other in disbelief.

"Walnut Street? Like the actual Walnut addition?" I asked.

Deborah pointed. "See? Right here. We can meet there after church."

I scoured the page. There had to be a catch.

After church, we headed to the neighborhood of our dreams. As we drove slowly past one beautiful home after another, Cindy said, "I feel like we're trespassing."

"I know. I feel it, too. What are we doing here? Who are we kidding?"

We knew we were out of our league until we came around a bend, and Cindy said, "Stop." She double-checked the address and pointed. "It should be right there."

We could see only dense trees and weeds. "That's it," she said, squinting.

We could barely make out a porch. "No wonder we've never noticed this place," I said.

Deborah suddenly appeared, dangling a house key. She led us through dense bushes to the front entrance. "Now, it needs a little fixing up," she said, using her shoulder to pop open the stubborn door.

Inside, our optimism quickly faded. We cautiously began our inspection, searching for glimmers of hope. Cindy moved right along, but I held back, overwhelmed by dingy neglect.

The dismal kitchen offered one glimmer of hope: a window that showcased a gorgeous view of trees and a charming house next door. This peaceful scene transfixed me until my eyes landed on a jarring sight. At the window next door, the glaring scowl of an elderly lady jolted me. Her stare clearly said, *Go. You don't belong here.*

Then Deborah walked in. "Oh, that's Lula."

"She looks angry."

"I'm sure she is. Since losing her husband a year ago, she's always complaining. The neighborhood association hears it all. I'm sure she's harmless."

I continued my disconcerting tour, and after seeing most of the house, I was ready to give this place the thumbs down. When I caught up with Cindy, she stood quietly staring at the fireplace. She reached out her hand and whispered, "Ethan."

"Yes?"

"This is it. This is our house."

Visions of a million fixes played through my mind. Then, for some inexplicable reason, I answered, "You're right." We were surrounded by wretchedness, yet something told me she was right.

Then peace came over me as Cindy pointed to the fireplace and said, "Big chair will go here, our oval rug there, and we'll sit by a warm fire."

I could see it. Then I joined in, saying, "You and the kids will decorate the Christmas tree there by the window."

The woeful house was showing us it still had joy in its bones. Cindy smiled, confirming that this would become our home.

Deborah zoomed by, holding her phone. "You guys keep looking. I've got to take this," She said, rushing outside.

I turned to Cindy. "So, this is really going to happen?"

"I'm sure God has brought us here."

I leaned against the fireplace, and a loose brick tumbled to the floor.

Cindy chuckled, "So you're starting the demo phase already?"

I laughed as I retrieved the brick and pretended to polish it before placing it back. "Wait, there's something in the hole." My keychain flashlight revealed a dingy piece of paper. "There's a note."

I extracted the yellowed note and tenderly unfolded it.

"What's it say?"

I held it to the light and read,

This home, completed on Thursday, the 10th day of July 1902, is hereby dedicated to the Lord God Almighty. Heavenly Father, hear our prayer. We stand within these walls you have provided and lift up our simple design to be greatly adorned with your love. May all who enter feel your presence and know your goodness. We welcome your holy angels.

"Ah ha! Look at that—angels," I said. Then I continued.

May they bring peace, protection, and abundant blessings to this home, now and forever. In his service.
–Rev. Ethan William Tettleton.

"It's a sign," Cindy said. "His name is Ethan, like yours. And he obviously has a thing for angels. It's meant to be."

"We should put this back. It belongs to the house."

"If we're going to buy this house, let's keep the letter," Cindy said.

"You're right."

"Just think. We're probably the first in over 100 years to see this letter. This house is meant for us. I just know it," Cindy said.

We hoped this would be the first of many miracles God had in store. So, despite its horrific condition, we fastened our seat belts and bit off the project that would push us to the edge. We had found a vintage house on Walnut Street that was in our price range. And though it was the smallest home in the neighborhood, it had plenty of space for us. I saw only two downsides: it needed work, and it needed *lots* of work.

We had much to learn, like how tricky it would be to purchase a vintage home. We applied for a loan, filled out lots of paperwork, and jumped through several hoops.

Just when everything was finally in place, Deborah called. "There's a snag," she said. "It's confusing, but apparently, the Property Owners Association has secured the property and has plans to bulldoze the house."

"What? What does that mean?" I said.

"The details are sketchy. Something about building a park. There's a meeting set for next week to clear things up. You need to be there."

We never saw this coming. It was time to pray and prepare our argument. And by meeting time, we were ready for battle.

Entering the meeting hall, I quickly spotted Lula's glaring face. "I think I know who's behind this mess," I whispered.

"Why would she do this?" Cindy said.

"Who knows? Did you bring our secret weapon?"

"It's right here," Cindy said, patting her purse.

Three board members sat at the front of the room. The meeting came to order as a silver-haired gentleman, whose nameplate read *Harold Harrington*, stood. "As some of you know, arrangements are being made with the National Parks Department and our property owners to convert the said property into a park. However, the Anderson family, who is here today, has placed an offer for the property."

Lula raised her hand and yelled, "Put on those slides again that show the deplorable condition of the property."

Mr. Harrington turned toward a young man with a laptop. "Okay, Robert, bring up the photos."

The lights dimmed, along with our hopes, as depressing photos garnered whispers among the members.

With the lights back on, I stood to talk. Cindy handed me the secret weapon, and I began presenting our case. "Thank you, property owners of Walnut Street, for agreeing to hear our case. My wife, Cindy, and I have admired Walnut Street for many years and dreamed we might live here someday. So, when the property seemed available, we offered to buy."

Lula's glare became more determined, but I kept my cool. "Yes, it's a fixer-upper, but we're up for the challenge." I opened our secret weapon and continued. "Here's a short letter discovered inside the house, hidden behind a fireplace brick for over 100 years. The original owner, Reverend Tettleton, wrote this as a prayer, dedicating the house to God in 1902."

I glanced across the room, avoiding Lula's face, and read the letter.

When I finished reading, the room remained quiet until Mr. Harrington said, "That's a very nice letter, Mr. Anderson, but I'm not entirely sure it has any bearing on this meeting."

Lula stood again, raising her hand, "Remember to tell everyone about the federal grant that will cover the upkeep and expenses for the park."

"Ethan, say something," Cindy whispered.

"What more can we say? It's their neighborhood, their choice."

$$\text{✗ ✗ ✗}$$

Driving home from the meeting, it was a beautiful sunny day, but Cindy's uproar blocked all of that. "Why do they need another park? Did they not like us? Why would God point us to that house if we can't have it?"

"I wish I could tell you."

"We need to go back to the house."

"Why torture ourselves?"

"It doesn't add up. We're missing something." Cindy said.

"Can't we just look for another place?"

"I'm not ready to give up. I'm calling Deborah."

I hated dragging out our disappointment, but there we were, parked in front of the house.

Deborah drove up, handing over the key. "Lock it up when you're done. I got to go,"

Cindy and I walked sadly toward the pitiful house.

As we reached the porch, shrouded by years of neglect, I said, "Maybe God has another place in mind."

Cindy looked upward and said, "Lord, please show us what we're missing."

"Sweetheart, I'm just not sure—"

"Wait," she said. "Did you hear that?"

We listened intently.

"Excuse me," a voice said as a heavyset man with a clipboard suddenly appeared from the side of the house. "Is this the Tettleton House?"

Cindy and I were bewildered. Did he know about the letter?

"I suppose you can call it that," Cindy said.

"Hi, I'm Sam Varney with the National Park Service. I'm preparing a report concerning the future park on this property.

I whispered to Cindy, "The homeowners don't waste time, do they?"

"Are you folks the owners of the property?"

"No, but we're trying to buy it."

Looking at his clipboard, Sam said, "The Walnut Street property owners seem to think it's theirs."

"Thanks to Lula," I said.

Sam turned, looking at the front door. "I would love to see inside."

"You're in luck," Cindy said, holding the key.

We were about to enter when Sam stopped to examine the area around the doorway. He grabbed a strand of overgrown ivy and yanked it from the wall.

"Ah ha, there it is," he said.

Putting on his glasses, he wiped debris from a nearly invisible brass plaque. He glanced at his clipboard and said, "This little beauty is an NRHP, and your plaque here confirms it." He could see our confusion and quickly added, "That's the National Registry of Historic Places."

"Is that a good thing?" Cindy asked.

"Yes. It means this house is historically significant." Then he smiled and patted the door frame. "According to our records, before any of these houses ever existed, Ethan Tettleton built this fine lady right here on these 640 acres?"

"This is the original house?" Cindy said.

"Yep, not only that, she's also a perfect historical example of style and materials for this region."

"So they can't bulldoze it?"

"Why would anyone want to do that?"

I glanced at Cindy and said, "It's our understanding the property owners want to clear off the house and make this a park."

"No. No. That's not how this works," Sam said. "Legally, the owners can demolish the house. But there goes its historical significance."

"So, if the house goes—"

"Yep, the historical value goes with it," Sam said.

⚔ ⚔ ⚔

For the next two days, we anguished over our next steps. The Property Owners Association would not return our calls. Then Mr. Harrington suddenly showed up at our door, holding a letter.

"Rather than mailing this, I decided to tell you in person."

"Uh oh, this sounds like bad news, I said.

"No, it's good news. You're cleared to proceed with your purchase. I just wanted to apologize on behalf of the board. We failed to do our homework. It was Lula's husband who envisioned the park project. After he died, Lula became determined to fulfill his wishes. Anyway, it's all in the letter," Mr. Harrington said as he walked away.

We opened the letter and read,

> *Our apologies for the opposition to your purchase of the property now known as the Tettleton House. The board and members are no longer interested in the park project and have cleared the way for your home purchase. Sorry for any inconvenience. Welcome to the neighborhood.*

Cindy smiled. "So, there it is—told you so. I just knew there was something special about that house."

We finally cleared the last hurdle and were handed the keys to our very own semi-dilapidated, historic home. We were staring at a lot of work but thrilled to be nestled among the most beautiful Victorian houses in town. And we had the very first one, the Grand Daddy of them all. That was indeed a God thing.

Cindy and I tried to shake the concern that something else might pop up to get us kicked out of the neighborhood, but at least we had keys to the property.

We filled boxes and loaded a large U-Haul. Then, with Dad's old pickup truck brimming with hand-me-down furniture, we carted all our worldly possessions toward Walnut Street. I'm sure we looked like junk dealers coming from the dump.

"Maybe we should wait till nightfall before we drive through Walnut Street," Cindy said.

"I thought about that, but I'm sure we can pull in, unload, and shove everything into the garage before anyone notices."

Entering the land of magnificent mansions, we tried to be discreet. But I imagined each stately home was filled with disgusted neighbors watching the riffraff move in.

We pulled into the driveway, and Cindy said, "How appropriate. The poor folks are moving into the eyesore house."

"Come on," I said. "This is the first step for turning the eyesore into the exquisite Tettleton House." She smiled at me as she put on her work gloves.

It took longer to unload our things than expected. With our pathetic belongings strewn about the driveway, I had to rest. I went to the porch, taking in our new view. Cindy came and put her arm around me. We stared directly across the street at the neighborhood's most gorgeous Victorian house.

"What must they be thinking right now?" I asked.

"There goes the neighborhood," she chuckled.

Just then, their front door flew open, and an older couple came out, headed straight toward us. "Yikes," I said. "I guess we're about to find out exactly what they're thinking."

Cindy and I stood our ground, ready to take the neighborhood disgust marching our way. The gentleman had heavy glasses, a stern expression, and a shirt that strained to hold his plump belly. The slender lady's face seemed hidden behind huge sunglasses.

"Oh boy, here it comes," Cindy whispered.

Suddenly, sternness turned into a warm smile as the man said, "Hi, folks. We're the Humphreys. Welcome to the neighborhood."

We were shocked. Then Cindy managed to say, "We're the Andersons, Cindy and Ethan."

"Hallelujah," Mrs. Humphrey said. "We are so glad to have new neighbors moving in."

"Really?" I said in disbelief. "We thought you might be neighborhood representatives coming to shoo us away."

"Certainly not," Mrs. Humphrey said. "We're excited to have new neighbors. Your charming house has sat empty for such a long time."

I glanced back at the house. "Yeah, the charm needs a lot of love."

Mr. Humphrey strained to peek inside our doorway. "She's in pretty rough shape, huh?"

"'Rough' is too kind a word, but we're up to the task—I hope."

"That's a shame about those last folks," Mrs. Humphrey said.

"Oh? We know nothing about them."

"A nice young family, until the husband went crazy and ran off chasing some odd dream."

"A dream?" I said.

"He was convinced that someday God would give him a million dollars. Then, one day, without explanation, he disappeared. No warning, no million dollars. The wife tried her best, but with two youngsters and an older house to maintain, she couldn't do it."

"That's so sad," Cindy said.

"We'll let you kids get back to it. Just wanted to say welcome."

Cindy and I watched as our new neighbors disappeared back into their splendid mansion.

"Well, Mrs. Anderson, looks like Walnut Street is officially our new home."

We pulled ourselves back to work, and by the end of that first day, we had neatly shoved everything we owned into the detached garage. Our empty house stood ready for the spectacular Anderson remodel.

8

The Worst Day

We had a simple plan: work at our jobs, then use every spare moment to renovate our new home. Lucky for us, Cindy's parents agreed to let us stay with them while we renovated.

On day two, we shoveled, swept, and scoured. As I carried the 12th trash bag to the curb, Mr. Humphrey was waiting. He looked quite serious as he handed me a business card that read *Junkinator Dumpster Service.*

"These guys are great," he said. "They bring a dumpster, you fill it, they haul it away."

In my tired state, this sounded wonderful. I fished out my phone and immediately scheduled a 15-footer. I hoped Cindy would be impressed.

Back inside, I found Cindy still sweeping. "Guess what. I ordered you a surprise."

She looked up from her broom and wiped her forehead with a gloved hand. "What is it?"

"It's a surprise. You'll get it tomorrow."

Not ready to play games, she just rolled her eyes. Then, dropping her broom, she headed to the front porch. I followed. She motioned for me to sit with her on the steps. "Want to hear something really crazy?" she said. "I think we should let tonight be the first night here in our new home."

"What? Look at this place. Your folks have planned for us to stay with them."

"I know. It's just that I can't wait to feel what it's like to live here."

She sounded like she had given it a lot of thought. "We'll need to retrieve some things from the garage," I said.

We opened the giant garage doors and dragged out our mattress, a lamp, and a moving box that would be our temporary nightstand. Soon, our bedroom had a cozy nest in the middle of the floor.

Later, as the night surrounded us, we lay listening for our new home to speak to us. The house offered a few creaks and groans, to which Cindy would smile as though her new home actually spoke.

"It's kind of like camping," I said.

"Listen. Can you feel it?"

"I feel a draft."

"No. The house, it's welcoming us."

"And you say I'm the odd guy?"

"It's like joyful whispers," she said. "The house is glad we're here."

I lay there trying to tune in. It was quiet at first, but then I noticed little sounds. I became aware of how the timbers and plastered walls surrounded us. I could see this house had been a home for so many families over many years, and now it was home for us. Cindy and I are part of a continuing story. I could finally feel a connection.

Laying flat on the floor, I knew I needed to experience this. If we were going to do this much work, we needed to find love for this house. The voice inside me whispered, "This is your place." I knew God meant our position in life along with this physical home. I welcomed his extraordinary gift, knowing that it would be his strength upon which we would restore this magnificent structure.

"You're right, Cindy. I do feel the connection. The story of this house continues now with our story."

"Yes, it's our place now," she said.

At that moment, everything felt right. We felt blessed with our new home. I turned off the lamp and held Cindy close.

Just as I drifted off, Cindy spoke. "Ethan, what is that?"

The concern in her voice forced me to sit up. The walls reflected a curious glow. I darted to the window. "Cindy! The garage is on fire!"

"Oh no! All of our things," she hollered, clambering for her phone.

I raced out the back door, certain all our belongings were about to be destroyed. I felt helpless. There was no water hose. What could I use? I spotted a plastic bucket and then searched for a faucet, but it was too dark. Then, I spotted an old kiddie pool full of murky water. I filled the drippy pail and barged through the garage side door—a big mistake. Air rushed in, and flames grew. My bucket was useless, and I slammed it down.

"Think, Ethan," I said, looking for anything to stop the fire.

Right then, water streamed from behind me. I turned to see Lula gripping her garden hose.

"Use this," she hollered.

I grabbed the hose. "Thanks, Lula. You gotta get out." She scampered away, and I attacked the flames. The inferno was relentless. Red hot debris fell on our belongings, cardboard boxes flamed, and smoke made it impossible to breathe.

I needed more than a scant stream of water. Then, out of nowhere, an immense blast of water and a voice shouting, "Get out! Now!" I turned, relieved to see a fireman's silhouette. I rushed past him, coughing my thanks.

"Anyone else?" he yelled.

"Just me."

I staggered out, glad to see two more firefighters jumping into action. Cindy ran to me, asking, "How could this happen?"

"I don't know." Then I looked at Lula's concerned face—so different from her angry glare. "Lula, thanks for your quick thinking. I don't know what I would have done without you."

"I'm sorry this is happening," Lula said.

The three of us stood there, bathed in the eerie light of a flashing truck and blistering flames. After one last fiery billow, the fire quickly died.

A tired fireman approached. "Worn out wiring," he said. "That's common with these old garages."

We were too in shock to have tears, but I knew they would come later. Everything we owned was now a pile of blackened, wet ashes.

Lula came to me. "I really must get back to Herby. Let me know what I can do to help. I'm right next door."

I never pictured I would do this, but I hugged her. "You really are an angel," I said. She gave a quick smile before scampering back to her home.

Under the worst circumstances, we discovered a beautiful neighbor who was no longer our scowling enemy.

Cindy and I stood quietly inspecting the damage as the truck pulled away. My keychain flashlight revealed a miserable pile of charred worldly goods. We had little hope that anything had survived.

I couldn't deal with any more of the catastrophe. "Let's get some rest and tackle things tomorrow."

When Cindy and I finally settled back into our mattress, we were exhausted but still wired from the night's tragic blow.

"What about our dishes?" Cindy said.

"Try not to think about it."

"Our Captain Double T-shirts? And Big Chair?"

Each item Cindy listed cut deeper into my heart. "We don't know anything for sure, and we really need to get some rest."

Then, she mentioned the one thing that would spur me into action.

"The Christmas Blanket?" she said.

I raised up. "Okay, let's go check the mess." We returned to the horror scene and opened the garage doors wide. The back porch floodlight reconfirmed our tragedy. We made our way into the mess, hoping to find surviving pieces, and by three o'clock, we were worn out. Everything seemed lost.

"Wait. Is that Big Chair?" Cindy said.

We peered deep into the clutter and recognized the arm of our beloved chair. I wrestled the beast from the scorched pile and dragged it into the light. We were speechless at the sight of our ruined best friend. Its charred remains were just one more disappointment that the last four hours had delivered. We were tired and grieving, which is a terrible combination.

I caught Cindy's eye and nodded toward the house. Her eyes agreed, and we retreated.

The following day, back on the driveway, daylight confirmed the devastation. Neither of us wanted to deal with it, so we just stood there like two sad statues. Then, out of the blue, we heard the loud screeches of a 15-foot dumpster unloading onto our driveway.

Cindy looked baffled.

"Oh, remember yesterday when I said I had a surprise for you?" I pointed to the dumpster. "Surprise!"

Shaking her head, Cindy said, "How are the two of us ever going to clean up this mess?"

"Good morning, my new neighbors." It was Lula coming our way, and she was not alone. "These are my grandsons, Tom and Bart."

The good-sized boys stood there quietly and did not look happy.

"I hope you don't mind. The boys said they wanted to help."

From their expressions, I doubted they wanted to help. Then Bart said, "Just tell us what you need us to do."

Cindy took charge, like being back at the cafeteria. "We need two piles: one for the salvageable and one for the dumpster." The boys put on their gloves and headed into the disaster.

As Cindy followed the boys, she suddenly stopped and looked back at me. She smiled lifting her palms upward and said, "I'm amazed. Here we are, facing our greatest tragedy, wondering how God could let this happen. And out of nowhere, we have two strong men and a beautiful dumpster. Go figure."

By mid-afternoon, the dumpster had captured mounds of ruined belongings. Then I saw Big Chair. His charred carcass peeked from the top of the dumpster as if bidding me farewell. "Goodbye, my old friend," I said under my breath.

It was hard to lose Big Chair, but what happened next was too much to bear. Bart came to me holding something. "I found a disintegrated box. Here's the only thing recognizable." He handed me a scorched piece of fabric.

I could see the image of a quilted dove and realized my worst fear. It was the Christmas Blanket.

"It's all burned up," he said.

I stared at the barely recognizable fragment, knowing I could not stand to see the rest. Cindy walked up and saw the scorched remnant. "Oh, my God. Is that—?"

I handed it to her. "It's my blanket."

Cindy looked around, and Bart pointed to a blackened heap by the dumpster. Cindy walked over to examine it. I watched her eyes comb through the contents. She suddenly covered her mouth with both hands and looked straight at me. Her tears said it all. The Christmas Blanket was gone.

I felt blood rush to my head as I marched toward the charred box. The fire that stole my Christmas blanket was now burning inside me. I grabbed the cursed bundle and slammed it hard into the dumpster. Its sickening thud would be my last interaction with the dear little Christmas blanket. I turned away, hiding my tears, and disappeared into the house to do whatever someone does when they suffer a profound loss.

And just like that, it was over. The wish, the miracle, the gift for a newborn king, all of it gone.

They said no one was killed in the fire, but I can say, with certainty, that a Bona Fide Christmas Expert died that day.

As my mind churned with sorrow, I heard Cindy enter the room. From behind, she wrapped her arms around me. I felt her tears through my shirt.

I'll make you a new one, she said.

I turned and held her tight. "I believe it was you who once told me there's only one Christmas blanket."

X X X

With the pain of the fire still heavy, we cleaned up the garage and tried to move on by immersing ourselves in the remodel.

Hard work seemed the only way to keep our minds from our tragedy. But I knew we were pushing ourselves too hard when a tired Cindy came to me saying, "Don't get me wrong. I love our Tettleton house, but let's leave off the Tettle and just call it Tons."

I was puzzled. "The Tons house?"

"It might as well be," she said. "This place is nothing but TONS of work."

She looked so serious, and I tried to hold it in, but I couldn't help but chuckle. Then, finally, she giggled, and all that stress we had been carrying gave way. We were both in tears, laughing. "Thank you. That's a pretty dumb joke, but I needed it," I said.

After months of hard work, the house finally showed some promise. Of course, it helped to have the Humphreys, my parents, Lula, and the not-so-friendly Tom and Bart all pitching in. We continued to work every spare moment and tackled every square inch, including plumbing and wiring— especially the wiring. The garage looked new, with its new roof, doors, and paint. Even our National Registry plaque was polished like new.

We were completely worn out when, one day, the last bit of construction dust got swept away, and we stood in the front yard admiring the fantastic transformation of our little Tettleton House. The Humphreys came over to join in our victory. "She's the finest house on Walnut Street," Mr. Humphrey said.

"Every house is the finest house," I said.

He leaned in and said, "I know, but now there's one more finest."

Our timing could not have been more perfect. We finished our remodel in time for the holidays and couldn't wait to decorate for our first Christmas at the Tettleton. And thanks to the Humphreys, our holidays got an early start.

"Hi, Andersons. Could you help us out?" Mr. Humphrey said. "We just got back from the Christmas tree farm, and somehow, they loaded two trees instead of one. Would you like to have a free Fraser Fir?"

"Yeah," Cindy said. "We'd love to have a free Fraser fir. That's a tongue-twister, isn't it?"

The Humphreys helped carry it inside to the ideal spot by our fireplace.

Anchored in its stand, we stepped back to admire it. Then, corny-me could not resist saying it. "First and foremost, it's a fortunate fluke to finally find a fine Fraser fir."

"For free." Cindy quickly added, rolling her eyes. "Oh my gosh, you're turning into my dad."

"On that note, we should probably go," said Mr. Humphrey. "Thanks for taking the fine Fraser off our hands."

Cindy hugged them and said, "I'm not sure this tree was accidental, but thank you for such a beautiful gift—our first tree in our new home."

"You're welcome," they said.

To see everything come together felt right. The tree and even our paltry furnishings made everything feel like home. Dad brought over some of their vintage ornaments, including bubble lights perfect for our historic Tettleton.

Standing in the freshly decorated living room, I waited for Cindy to happen by. When she finally entered the room, she could read my expression. "What are you up to? You look guilty."

My eyes kept darting to the fine Frazier Christmas tree. Cindy quickly spotted the beautifully wrapped present at its base.

"What's that?"

I just smiled, which coaxed her to check it out.

She shook it, smelled it, and said, "It's kinda early for presents."

"Not really," I said. "In fact, today is an excellent day for this."

She carefully unwrapped it, revealing a framed letter.

"The secret weapon! You framed the Tettleton prayer," she said. "It looks beautiful."

"After a hundred years stuck behind a brick, it's time to show it off."

"Reverend Tettleton would be proud of this moment," she said.

"Yes, he would."

"Where shall we put this?"

"There's really only one place, don't you think?"

Cindy walked to the fireplace and placed it on the mantel. "Oh, Ethan, that's perfect."

"It's a national treasure—right where it belongs."

Cindy gave me her pixie smile. "I think today might be an excellent day for another gift. Come with me." We walked to the driveway. "Face that way, and don't peek."

I covered both eyes. "A new car?" I said.

"Even better. Ready?"

"Of course."

"Merry Christmas, Ethan."

I turned around and couldn't believe it. "Is that—"

"Yes, it is. The one and only," she said.

"Big Chair!" I hollered. "I can't believe it. He was all burned up, hauled off in the dumpster."

"Not exactly hauled off. Mr. Humphrey spotted Big Chair and told me he had a guy—a real furniture genius."

I walked closer for inspection. Big Chair looked perfect, exactly like before, only newer.

"Now for the proper test," I said, sitting nice and slow. Cindy waited anxiously for my verdict. "Ah, my old friend is back."

"Yes!" she said, hopping on my lap like old times.

And so, Big Chair resumed his proper place in our home and in our hearts. The world felt right again ... well, almost.

❄ ❄ ❄

Everything was coming together, and I was confident this year's wish vigil would be the one, even without the blanket. And when our first Walnut Street Christmas Eve arrived, Cindy and I stayed up together for the wish. Being her first vigil, she felt a little nervous.

"So, what do I do when the angel shows up? Will you simply disappear? See ya later? Watch out for camels?"

Cindy got me thinking. Other than Grandma Ada, I'd never shared my wish vigil. "Honestly, I don't know," I said. "I've never thought about it."

"Well, if it's all the same to you, I'd like to go to bed and leave it with you and the angel."

"Probably a good idea."

Cindy was not surprised that by 12:15, I was coming to bed with no angel and no wish.

"Next year," Cindy whispered.

Apparently, God had not found me to be ready because the next year and plenty of years that followed yielded the same disappointing results. But I couldn't shake Grandma Ada's words: *One day, you'll hear an angel's song and know you're ready for the wish to come true.* What song? What angel? All I ever learned was that I'm just not ready.

❦ ❦ ❦

Our Tettleton House blessed us in many ways, but maybe we needed one or two more blessings. Cindy and I both wanted to have children. "If it happens, it happens" became our philosophy.

And one day, Cindy said, "It's happening." God blessed us with a baby boy. We named him James.

When I first saw James, I was thankful that God would trust me with this fantastic new life. I studied his beautiful little face, eyes, and soft skin for hours. Is this what it will be like when I finally see the infant Jesus lying in the manger?

I gracefully danced across the room with tiny James in my arms. "Look,

Cindy, we made a human."

She chuckled. "I think God had something to do with it."

"You're right. It takes three to make a baby."

The miracle of life had us spellbound. Then, 17 months later, another blessing arrived with our daughter, Shelly. Her beautiful blue eyes filled us with joy. She was our little angel, so sweet. And as kids tend to do, our kids quickly grew, and we became the perfect little family, living in the perfect little house.

It's almost funny when everything seems right; a single phone call can turn everything upside down.

9

Too Much a Bother

It was late afternoon when Dad called. "I just talked with Ada's doctor, and it's what we thought. The signs are all there." Dad's voice rarely sounded so disheartened.

"I'm so sorry," I said.

"She can't live by herself anymore," he said.

"Is there a facility?"

"No. None of us want that. And our house is way too small."

Dad's drift was obvious. I hesitated, which made it awkward, then said, "Well, we have a bedroom."

"Yeah?"

"I'll talk to Cindy."

I gathered my thoughts and finally approached Cindy. "Dad called."

"I know. Your Mom called me, and I have mixed feelings."

"Me too, but what else can we do?"

Cindy shook her head. "How will her living here affect the kids?"

"Dad says she is sometimes confused but mostly quiet."

"I know we have a bedroom, but I'm just not sure about this?"

"Ada has always been there for everyone. I remember all the great times spent with her." I paced the room. "Mom and Dad will help, and the kids will adapt. I can't turn my back when she needs us."

"You're right," Cindy said. "God did bless us with this house."

We agreed to the arrangement, and the next day, Dad's pickup came backing into our driveway. Grandma's belongings streamed in, making a tidy stack of boxes in her new room. Mom and Dad unpacked and arranged things as Grandma quietly watched.

I sensed her anxiety and whispered to Cindy, "Grandma doesn't need to watch this. Let's take her for a drive."

With our newest household member, the five of us toured around town, driving to places I hoped Grandma would recognize. But her thoughts were on just one thing. "I hope I'm not too much a bother."

"Grandma, you're our family. We want you to be with us."

We continued our relaxing drive until Grandma pointed and hollered, "Stop the car!"

"What is it?"

"Over there," she said, pointing to the cemetery.

I pulled into River Valley Cemetery. Grandma climbed out of the car and scurried past a sign that read *Trinity Gardens.*

"Stay here, guys," I said.

I followed Grandma along a stone path until she stopped and leaned close to a headstone. I gave her a moment before walking up.

Grandma wiped her tears as she quickly headed back toward the car. I examined the headstone, which read,

Beloved

Ellie Anderson

Born on Easter

April 5, 1931 • Died April 5, 1931

We were quiet for our drive back home. Mom and Dad greeted us and took Grandma to see her room.

Cindy asked me, "What was that about at the cemetery?"

"I'm not sure. There's a grave marked Ellie Anderson. She died at birth.

"Oh, Ethan, who could that be?"

"I've never heard of her,"

We went inside and found the room looking remarkably like Grandma's home. She smiled with awareness as she discovered her things nicely arranged in the warm, inviting space. Cindy gave me a peaceful smile that confirmed we were doing the right thing.

I walked Mom and Dad to their truck. "Dad?" I said.

"What is it, son?"

I wanted to ask about the grave. But instead, I said, "You guys did a great job with Grandma's room. I think she's going to be happy here."

"Thank you, son. I know it's a big undertaking. We appreciate what you and Cindy are doing for Mom."

🦋 🦋 🦋

We quickly adjusted to our new family dynamic. I loved having little talks with Grandma, even though I did most of the talking. We took her on short neighborhood walks where every house we passed became her favorite.

One day, as we chatted in her room, she caught me off guard. "Where is the Christmas Blanket?"

I struggled for words and finally said, "I haven't seen it lately."

"I would love to see it again."

How could I tell her that her beautiful Christmas blanket was incinerated and buried in a landfill?

With that thought, I began having doubts concerning the wish. Could it ever be fulfilled with no blanket and Grandma in her condition?

"Look at all the pretty ribbons," Grandma said, gazing at her wall of multicolored award ribbons.

"Those are state fair ribbons you won for all the beautiful things you've made."

"Well, of course. That's what those are," she said.

I was very familiar with her ribbon collection, having watched it grow through the years. Grandma once told me how she had finished my blanket in time to enter it at the fair, and it had won a blue ribbon.

Years ago, I asked Grandma how she could win so many ribbons for the things she made. "Honey, I simply make everything as though I'm making it for Jesus himself. I imagine him watching as I create it, and when I've finished, I hand it to him in my heart. And it's funny how my little projects always seem to turn out pretty good. At least, most folks seem to like them."

"Whatever you do, work at it with all your heart,
as working for the Lord."
– Colossians 3:23 (NIV)

Grandma had a special connection with the Savior. I remembered how some of that connection would rub off on me whenever I held my little Christmas Blanket. It was as though I could feel the presence of Jesus by merely running my fingers over the delicate needlework. This feeling had always been strongest on Christmas Eve. But now, the blanket is gone.

Having Grandma with us brought bittersweet moments. The kids adapted much better than expected. They never noticed if Grandma was having a good day or bad; they just saw Grandma.

I walked by her room once and found four-year-old Shelly having a tea party with Ada. Her little tea set barely fit on Grandma's side table.

"Grandma, would you like some more tea?" I heard no response. "Is that enough? And Miss Lamby, would you like some too?" Shelly was having a wonderful time and had no problem with unresponsive Grandma. She just liked being with her.

I, on the other hand, could remember the Ada who would relish a tea party as lovely as this. In fact, I've witnessed many tea parties where Susie and Gail happily played with their exuberant grandmother.

Having a front-row seat for watching Grandma slip away was more challenging than I expected. Each day, as her mind faded, my joy faded too. It was like a blanket of sadness was being draped over me.

Cindy could see I was hurting. Then, one day, she was suddenly standing in front of me. "I think I'm supposed to tell you something."

"What's that?"

"The holidays are near. Let's decorate Ada's room for Christmas."

"Sounds good to me," I said, hoping it might cheer me as much as Ada.

We dug out Ada's decorations, starting with her silver tree. "Look at these handmade decorations," Cindy said, opening an old box.

"I remember those," I said, lifting delicate memories from the box. "These are the ones made by all the cousins. I can't believe she still has them."

We decorated the tree and even had James and Shelly add new homemade treasures. Soon, the familiar groan of Grandma's colorful light wheel filled us with nostalgic delight. It felt good seeing it back in action.

We had done our best to make the space Christmassy like her sunroom, but where was that familiar amber glow? I found her antique lamp in the attic and placed it beside her bed. The instant I turned it on, Ada gave me a little smile. Her room now felt complete.

Moments like this boosted my outlook. But even small reminders of Grandma Ada's condition could slam me into darkness.

❌ ❌ ❌

When Christmas Eve arrived, the wish seemed impossible. How could it ever happen without the Christmas Blanket and Grandma in her dim condition? I had to remind myself that the wish would be God's miracle, and he could make it happen. So, as midnight neared, I joined Ada in her room and fought the heaviness of a hopeless wish.

As I waited for the midnight chimes, I noticed Cindy suddenly standing in the doorway. Something was wrong. She was on the verge of tears.

"Remember our first night in this house? Cindy said. "How we slept on the floor?"

"Of course, I remember."

"And we brought some things from the garage, a mattress, and a lamp?"

"Yeah."

"And a moving box to use as a nightstand?"

"That sounds right."

"I never looked inside that box," she said, with tears glistening. "Until now."

I tried to make sense of what was happening. Then, from behind, Cindy slowly revealed an unbelievable sight—the Christmas Blanket.

"What? How can this be?" I jumped up to see.

Cindy struggled to speak. "Ethan, it's your Christmas blanket."

I held it up, scanning every star, tree, dove, and the beautiful angel, even Grandma's tiny cross. It was all there, in perfect condition.

"But the fire. We saw it destroyed."

"You saw Ada's quilting scraps. Remember? She brought them to teach me how to quilt." I embraced Cindy and said, "Of all those boxes we stored in the garage, God saved one—this one."

Grandma suddenly spoke. "There it is," she said, pointing at the blanket.

I handed it to her. "Look, Grandma, it's the Christmas Blanket. And it's Christmas Eve. It's time for our wish to come true."

With perfect timing, the clock chimes began. "I'll leave you two alone," Cindy said as she disappeared down the hallway.

Was this really happening? Surely, the blanket's well-timed return meant we were ready. I prepared myself as each chime drew me closer to the wish. My mind was again filled with images of angels, starlight, and the manger. The last chime sounded. Would this be the wondrous, wish-fulfilling moment at last? Echoes of the twelfth chime were fading in my ear. Not breathing, I stood to my feet, anticipating a holy visitor.

Then I heard a sound from behind. A soft voice that said, "I'm here."

My body stiffened, and my eyes grew wide. This was it. The wish was beginning. I turned slowly and found my six-year-old son James standing sleepily in his pajamas. I quickly regained my "Daddy" composure, and with an enormous sigh, I leaned down and held James by his little shoulders.

"Yes, I guess you are here," I said.

"I thought you were Santa Claus."

"Oh, James. Come and let me tell you a little story about Grandma Ada."

I wrapped the blanket around James, and we sat beside Grandma's bed. As she slept, I told him about our special Christmas wish: the angel, the Nativity, and the star shining down. I knew he enjoyed the story when he declared, "I love that wish."

"Me too," I answered. "Me too."

I gave James a big kiss and pointed him toward his room. "It's off to bed for the both of us." I proclaimed.

As I ambled down the hall, reality set in. Has anyone ever traveled back in time? Was this wish thing just the silly imaginings of an overgrown kid? I felt foolish, yet my peculiar little thoughts kept bubbling up from the same part of my soul that believes in angels, miracles, and the Christ child who was born to save us from sin.

I don't think I've been some weirdo who obsesses about miracles or gets caught up in magical thinking. Surely, I'm just an ordinary guy with a regular job, a great family, and fun hobbies. It's just that I had always felt something was missing from the wish. Grandma always said God would know when we were ready.

It was an undeniable feeling that nudged me toward the wish whenever I held that soft little blanket.

I may not have been ready all these years, but I have always loved the peaceful moments right around midnight each Christmas Eve. And now, the Christmas Blanket has returned.

10

Struggling

"Ethan, why are you having to work late every night?"

Down deep, I knew it was to avoid Grandma's long goodbye.

Cindy could see it, too, so she found clever ways to cheer me up. Her best attempt happened one Halloween when she walked by wearing a Captain Hubble t-shirt. "Happy Halloween," she said, performing an exaggerated runway walk.

"What's this? I thought our shirts were destroyed."

"Found it online," she said, tossing me a duplicate shirt. "Captain Double lives."

Her cleverness worked. I was actually laughing as we reminisced about our first date. I was even about to growl the catchphrase, but Cindy put her finger to my lips, "Nope," she said.

James walked by. "What's that?" he said.

"It's Halloween. We're dressed up as Captain Double. Pretty scary, huh?" Cindy said.

"Can I wear one?" James asked.

Cindy smiled at me. "What do you think? We could be Captain Triple."

"We have to go all the way with the Captain Quadruple," I said.

"Oh, that would be so cute. Next year, we're totally doing that."

Later that day, Cousin Gail suddenly appeared at our door holding a sack.

"Hey, Miss Chicago. Did you get homesick?"

"You goofball. You know I always come back for Halloween."

"Oh yeah."

"Plus, my old journalism professor asked me to speak to his class."

"I'm impressed."

"Meh," she said, rolling her eyes. Then she reached into her sack. "I have something for you." She handed over a small wooden box. "Ada gave me this when I moved to Chicago, and I have absolutely no use for it."

"I've seen this before."

"It's her recipes. Like I'm ever gonna cook."

Opening the box revealed a well-used collection of hand-written recipes. I lifted a random card and read, *Aunt JoAnn's Carrot Cake.*

"I remember that one. It's good," Gail said.

"Cindy will love these recipes. Are you sure you don't—"

"Oh, God, no. Please take 'em."

Gail looked around the room. "So, how's Grandma these days?"

"Come see for yourself."

We crept down the hallway and peeked into her room. "Hello, Grandma, it's me, Gail." Grandma mustered a well-timed, coherent moment as she reached toward Gail and smiled. Gail gave her a kiss.

"My little Gail, all grown up," Grandma said.

"I think you just made her day."

Gail stood quietly, watching as Grandma's smile faded and her eyes drifted shut. "And, there she goes," Gail said. "Does that happen a lot?"

"It's typical."

Gail glanced around Grandma's room and sighed. Then, we headed back to the living room. "How do you do it, Ethan? How do you keep from getting depressed?

"Who says I'm not depressed?"

"You and Grandma always had a special bond." Then, with a little chuckle, she asked, "So, did you and Grandma ever go back in time?"

"Not yet."

"Not yet? You mean you still think it's going to happen?"

"Of course not." It surprised me how those words rolled out so easily. Was I no longer able to stand up for the wish?

"That wish was all you could talk about. Wanna know why your wish has never come true? Because the Nativity never happened. At least not like the fairy tale the Bible tells. They just fabricated some grandiose story they borrowed from the Pagans."

I couldn't take any more of Gail's cynicism. I had to switch topics. "So, do you still have the Thanksgiving Blanket?"

"Mom, has it packed away somewhere. I saw the Christmas Blanket in Grandma's room."

"Yeah, it's one of the things she can remember."

Gail scrutinized the living room. "Looks like you're an adult now with a real grown-up house. Isn't it good to get past all that lame childhood stuff?" She said.

"As I recall, you couldn't wait to be a grown-up."

"Come on. We both know I was born a grown-up," she said, glancing at her watch. "Speaking of which, I should get back for another stupid class."

"Thanks for the recipes."

"You're welcome. Save me a slice of carrot cake."

As Gail flew out the door, a streak of disappointment swept through me. I had wimped out concerning the wish. It was not that I failed to defend it.

It was that, for a fleeting moment, I failed to believe it. Something was happening to me.

❆ ❆ ❆

I must have spent lots of time sitting in Big Chair with my withering spirit on display because Cindy made more attempts to brighten my mood. This time, it was early Christmas shopping.

"We have lots of nieces and nephews to buy for," Cindy said.

"Does it have to be today?"

"You're the Christmas guy. You've always loved picking out the kid's presents."

That year, the massive toy store felt overwhelming. My shopping cart had a wobbly wheel, and after wobbling through the entire store, Cindy pointed to our cart and asked, "Is that all we're giving the kids this year?"

I stared at the meager gathering. Then my frustration grabbed a nearby plush bear and threw it in the cart.

"Stop it," Cindy said.

"Okay. Let's get this over with."

That evening, with gloomy eyes again fixed on the fireplace, my jacket suddenly landed in my lap. "Let's take an evening walk," Cindy said.

The thought of a walk made me feel heavy and tired.

"Ethan, The world's most beautiful setting is just outside our front door."

As I lumbered out of the chair, Cindy examined me and asked, "Why are you wearing that shabby sweater?"

I looked at myself. "Who cares?"

Cindy shook her head, and then she opened the front door. "Christmas on Walnut Street, here we come."

We stepped into a dazzling Christmas setting. Colorfully lit Victorian homes resembled a movie set. As we strolled, Cindy pointed to the stately homes. "Aren't you glad we found this?" I struggled to be in the moment and see it as she sees it.

"Ethan, all that work we did wasn't easy, but look at this magical place."

"It's nice," I said.

Cindy took my hand. "I know you're having a hard time. You're missing Grandma, the way she used to be. I am, too."

I was trying hard not to spoil Cindy's joy.

She stopped and put her arms around me. Her touch tried to warm my mood. If a photographer came by, they would have found a lovely scene with two lovers silhouetted against a festively lit Victorian manor adorned with just the right amount of snow. That's what Cindy was seeing. But I saw myself as a dark figure surrounded by gray coldness while a few miserable Christmas lights tried to cheer me up. I could not find the part of me that loved moments like this.

As we returned home, Big Chair and the Christmas Blanket were posing next to our twinkling tree. This sight had always triggered joyful thoughts concerning the wish, but something had drained their meaning. I suddenly saw the wish as a mere indulgence that edified only me. Could it be that I'd never be ready until the wish meant more than my selfish desire?

🜚 🜚 🜚

It became a habit. After so many years of failed wish vigils, it was now my tradition to go through the motions. So it was no surprise that as the next Christmas Eve arrived, I mindlessly began prepping for the vigil. I knew how it would play out, but, of course, I had to try.

At 11:30 p.m., I peeked into Grandma's room. "Hi, Grandma. It's Christmas Eve."

Grandma stared at the wall.

"Remember our wish? Maybe it will come true tonight." She remained still as I spoke. "It's all your fault. The wish started with you." I leaned forward, elbows on my knees. "You had a way with us grandkids. You taught us so much about Jesus. Remember your outdoor Nativity scene? I still think about that night you joined me outside years ago." Grandma looked at me, showing no emotion.

"Tonight is Christmas Eve. Are we ready for the angel to appear?"

With no expression, Grandma turned back to the wall, and everything about the wish collapsed. We were supposed to be the wish team. To witness the Nativity together and give baby Jesus the Christmas Blanket. Had the wish faded away? Maybe that's what wishes are, just little glimpses of hope or pathetic dreams that wither and die.

I hung my head, feeling the onslaught of reality. Yet a tiny part of me still clung to that wish, like a small flickering candle in the dark. I imagined the midnight chimes might miraculously cause Grandma to snap out of it. That she would again be herself, eager to receive our precious wish. An angel would appear and lead us on our miracle journey.

Then, reality surged again as Grandma suddenly groaned with pain.

"Grandma? Are you all right?"

She closed her eyes and returned to a peaceful slumber. I knew there would be no angel on this night.

How long would I cling to this stupid wish? Then, for the first time, I chose not to conduct the wish vigil. I drifted to the bedroom, where Cindy lay fast asleep, unaware that a sad quitter was crawling in bed. My silent prayer that night was an apology to God for my ridiculous wish. I then fell into a deep sleep.

It was the middle of the night when I woke up. How strange, I could see Grandma standing in our bedroom. "Our wish is real," she said, pointing to Heaven. "It will happen." Then, she just vanished.

I hurried to her room and found her sleeping. Had this been a dream? Her words still resonated in my ear, and anxious thoughts kept me awake for the rest of the night.

$$\text{\Large \Yup \quad \Yup \quad \Yup}$$

Over the next dreadful months, life with Ada became unbearable. Not that she was any trouble; I just felt helpless and angry about the dimming of her life.

Her condition steadily worsened until one cold fall night, I had to get out of the house. I walked down the street to Walnut Park. My mind was churning as I wandered among the ancient trees. The night breeze, full of falling leaves, encouraged my emptiness. I stopped and looked up at dark branches that clawed against the gray sky.

"God, where are you?" I moaned. "Where is your comfort in this valley of the shadow of death? "This is wrong—so wrong." Then I just stood there feeling numb. Maybe I expected God's voice to warm my heart, but he seemed so far away.

I finally trudged back home and peeked in on Ada. She was awake, and I tried to capture her attention, but she just stared into a dark corner. As I had often done before, I just began talking, mainly about my childhood experiences with her.

During our one-sided conversation, I could feel my outrage flaring. Enough was enough. I could no longer contain the anger. I made it to the hallway, seething with rage, and knew there was no stopping the storm inside. *This can't be me,* I thought as I lost control.

Shaking both fists toward Heaven, I yelled, "God, tell me why. Ada had such faith in you. Everything she did, everything she made, was for you. How could you take away her mind and her memories?" I fell to my knees. "The stupid wish is just a joke. I thought you were a loving God—the light of the world—the God who heals. Are you even real?"

A hand touched my shoulder, and I heard Ada's trembling voice, "Ethan, he is real." I turned. Her pleading eyes locked onto mine. Then, to my horror, she collapsed to the floor.

"Grandma!" I reached and held her frail body. "Cindy! Call for help."

Grandma moved her lips, and I could barely make out her words. "You know he is real."

"Yes, Grandma. I know he's real. I know. I know."

Her body fell limp, and in that instant, she was gone.

"Oh, God, how could you allow this? All she wanted was to serve you— to see you."

11

Total Darkness

It's hard to talk about this chapter in my life, but I must tell it.

I could not imagine what epitaph might ever be written for such a beautiful person. Are mere words enough?

On the day of Grandma Ada's funeral, my grief was trying to find its place, but anger left very little room.

Walking into the chapel, I spotted her coffin nestled among a forest of floral arrangements. There was fabric draped across her stately casket. Squinting revealed it was the four baby blankets she made for her grandchildren. It was such a fitting tribute to her love for others. Seeing these blankets displayed for her last farewell comforted me.

We found our place in the family section—the sad section. As I took my seat, Cousin Rickey leaned in. "Can you believe I actually found my blanket?"

Then Susie whispered, "I believe I'm the one who found both blankets."

I smiled. "They're a beautiful sight."

Grandma's service was nice. The Pastor had many pleasant things to say, but nothing conveyed what Grandma Ada was truly about. When the Pastor had finished, he asked if anyone would like to share a word about Ada.

Everyone remained still, and just as the silence became awkward, I surprised myself by standing. What was I doing?

I felt everyone's eyes follow me to the pulpit. I stood at the microphone with nothing prepared. Looking across the church, I was amazed by the many lives she had touched.

I prayed silently, *God, whatever I'm about to say will have to be all you because I've got nothing.*

I took a deep breath and peered at the casket. "Wow, Grandma, you sure know a lot of people." I then felt God's nudging and continued. "My Grandma Ada was a wonderful lady. Of course, I would say that since I'm her grandson. But I can prove it. Just look around. So many marvelous people are packed in here today. You wouldn't be here if she wasn't wonderful. It only makes sense when you spend a lifetime loving, caring, and making things to give away that people will remember. She never cared about a person's social status, politics, or age. She just saw a person whom God created and placed in her path. That's all it took for her to look into your eyes and connect."

I glanced at the cousins. "It was an absolute joy to have Ada as a grandmother, right, Gail? Rickey? Susie? She could take anything and make it memorable and fun. Grandma loved to decorate her yard for Christmas. I'm sure Papa Nate was not happy having to put up so many lights. But he knew better than to argue with Ada. Down deep, I know he loved seeing all the beautiful decorations and the joy they brought. I remember when she added a Nativity scene. The glowing figures reminded me of the real meaning of Christmas. Grandma joined me out in the cold one Christmas Eve. Standing by her nativity scene, she pointed to the smallest figure and began teaching me about Jesus. It felt like the two of us were there at the actual Nativity. She never missed an opportunity to talk about Him."

I could see agreeing faces in the crowd, and I continued. "I'm sure Ada has taught everyone in this room about Jesus. That's what she did. That's who Ada was. And now, she's standing next to him, her Lord and Savior. But hey, we already knew that, didn't we? We love you, Ada Anderson."

After I paused for a moment, more words came to me, "We praise and thank you, Father, for the glorious life of Ada Anderson."

I retreated from the microphone, contemplating the words I had just spoken. I needed to hear them, but my anger still simmered.

The graveside service happened under dark clouds. The four cousins gathered near the casket, each holding our own blanket. We bowed, but my heavy thoughts drowned out the closing prayer. Then it was done. It was time to go home and deal with grief.

Cindy took my hand and gave me a sad smile. "It's going to be okay."

I kissed her on the forehead. Then I noticed Mom and Dad standing at a nearby grave.

"Cindy, wait here a moment."

Dad spotted me as I approached. "Did you know you had a great-aunt?"

"I had my suspicions," I said.

"Ellie Anderson was Ada's twin sister who died at birth."

"A twin? No one ever told me."

"I know. It was something we never talked about. It was Mom's secret sorrow. She came here often and never talked about her."

☥ ☥ ☥

For several days after the funeral, memories of Grandma flooded my thoughts. But even happy memories could not stop my dark mood. I'm sure it was because of this newcomer called grief. It was hard to lose Papa Nate and now Grandma, for they had fostered my sense of wonder.

I put it off for at least a week before venturing into Grandma's room. The dark emptiness fueled my sorrow. I looked around, wishing she would walk in and sit with me.

Cindy walked in and turned on the lights. "How are you holding up?"

I tried to find an answer.

"Can you talk about it?" she asked.

I peeked into my feelings and said, "I feel like a little boy who spends hours building a tall tower with toy blocks. I'm so proud of that tower. Then, for no reason, it collapses. What happened? There must be someone to blame. And now, as I look at the scattered blocks, I'm mad and confused."

"Okay. That's a little weird, even for Odd Guy," Cindy said.

"I know, but it's the same feeling I get every Christmas when I'm hoping for a miraculous wish that never happens. I'm just not ready for the wish or any of this." I scanned the room, "Cindy, look around. Nothing but dashed hopes—scattered blocks. And no one to blame, just me."

Cindy's frustration was evident as she moved toward the door. "None of this is your fault."

We stared at each other for a moment. "So, what do we do with all this?" I said, gesturing at Grandma's belongings.

"Someone will have to sort through it. You should look and see what you're dealing with," she said, walking away.

I surveyed the room, noticing dresser drawers, boxes, and a full closet. And in the corner, a hope chest I recognized from years ago. Feeling curious, I tugged on its aged cedar lid. Inside were pieces of tired fabric and an ancient cardboard box underneath. I opened its yellowed lid, revealing a handmade blanket. What is this? I studied it briefly, then carefully lifted it to the bed for closer inspection. It was well-preserved and quite beautiful. Its images depicted Easter with lilies, palm fronds, and Jesus on the cross. It was unfinished.

"Cindy. You need to see this," I hollered.

"What?" Cindy said, peeking into the room. Then she saw the blanket. "Oh my God, what is that?"

"Grandma never showed us this."

Cindy tenderly examined the box's contents and then spotted a note. "Perhaps this will tell us something." She carefully unfolded the aged letter and read,

To my dear sweet Easter babies. I'm sorry that my body was not strong enough. Ada, my beautiful baby girl, you are alive with me, and I love you dearly. Ellie, your sweet life was cut short so that Ada could live. Death took you from this life to a better life with Jesus. I love and miss you very much. When you both were as one inside me, I made your baby blanket. It's for Easter and tells the story of God's mighty love. But you came before I could finish. I will leave it unfinished as a symbol of the hole in my heart. I will carry the emptiness until that day when I see you again.

Dabbing her eyes with a tissue, Cindy said, "So strange that Ada never mentioned this."

"I'm sure Grandma knew we would find it someday."

Cindy caressed the blanket and said, "So beautiful. And so sad."

This Easter Blanket must have been my tipping point as strange dreams began invading my sleep. There was one dream involving the Christmas Blanket that really shook me. I was walking in a vast desert. In the distance, I saw a spindly tree with something hanging from its branches. Stepping closer, I recognized the Christmas Blanket. It upset me to see it twisted and dangling there. Then, the strangest thing happened, the Blanket spoke.

"Ethan, why do you hate me?"

I tried to say I could never hate something so wonderful, but when I spoke, my words came out saying, "I hate you because you broke your promise." What was I saying? These can't be my words.

"Why do you deserve my promise?"

I cried out, "You lied. You promised." My rage erupted, and I wanted to destroy the Blanket. I grabbed it and threw it to the ground. Then I stomped it in the dirt. My beautiful Blanket was being destroyed, and I couldn't stop it.

"No," I screamed. "You're supposed to be a wonderful gift meant for Jesus." At my feet lay the destroyed blanket. I lifted it and saw blood dripping. I cried out, "What have I done?"

Then I was awakened by Cindy's touch. "Ethan, what's wrong?"

Still filled with emotion, I got up. "I'm okay. Go back to sleep."

I was not okay. I went to the living room and found the blanket resting on Big Chair. I embraced it and whispered, "I don't deserve your promise. I don't deserve the wish."

❊ ❊ ❊

With my Christian upbringing, I should have been a super-Christian, leading Bible studies and feeding the hungry. But it was a numbness that filled me. I had slid off the playing field and didn't care. I knew my pain was tearing at the family.

"Look, Daddy. I drew a doggy," Shelly said, handing me a crayon-laden sheet of paper.

"That's nice," I said without really seeing.

"I made it for you because Mommy said you're sad."

"I'm okay, Sweetie. Thank you for the nice picture."

As Shelly turned away, she carried a bit of my gloom with her.

The following day, on my way to the coffee pot, the sight of the Christmas Blanket halted me. I just stared at it, remembering the comfort it once gave. But I could no longer trust that feeling. The blanket that had always brought joy now delivered sorrow.

It was time to do something. I folded it neatly and wrapped it in a plastic bag. Cindy was at the end of the hallway as I pulled down the attic stairs. She watched me carry the blanket into the darkness. Then, without words, she turned to leave.

"Aren't you going to say something?" I said.

She turned back and asked, "Is it over?"

"I don't know. There's something different about the blanket."

"I mean the wish. Have you given up on it?"

I had no answer. The blanket's ability to keep the wish alive had faded. Maybe it was time to grow up and leave the wish in my childhood where it belonged. My vigil suddenly felt small. I finally saw a grown man's ridiculous belief in an impossible wish. The Christmas Blanket had always been an essential part of the wish, and now it was packed away. "God, you have shown me my foolishness. I repent for holding the wish as something dear."

I carried my coffee and heavy thoughts to the front porch, seeking solace in our incredible view. Leaning against the porch post, I stared at the beauty that lived all around me. That's when Lula walked by. She waved and came toward me. "Ethan. How are you this morning?"

I wanted to sound cheerful but could only say, "I'm not sure."

"I'm sorry to hear about your grandmother. I sometimes saw Ada at the grocery store; she was always so nice."

"I had no idea you knew her."

"It's a small world," she said.

It surprised me when she said, "I've been thinking about you lately, and a Bible verse keeps popping up. Psalm 40:1-2, I wrote it down since I can't memorize like I used to."

She handed me a piece of paper, and I read it out loud,

> *"I waited patiently for the Lord; he inclined to me and heard my cry. He drew me up from the pit of destruction, out of the miry bog, and set my feet upon a rock, making my steps secure."*

"Give it some thought. Let me know if any of that makes sense for you," she said, walking away.

I was definitely in a pit of destruction and a miry bog. I felt encouraged by Lula's scripture, but the storm inside me was stubborn.

A few days later, Gail, who never called ahead, appeared again at our door.

"Hello, Gail."

Her expression seemed strange. "Cindy called. She's worried about you."

"She's worried I'm going to Hell."

"Are you?"

"At times, it feels like I'm already there."

"Is this about losing Grandma? Because if it is, you need to get over it."

"I don't know. Nothing seems important anymore."

"Nothing? Your family? Your work? That wish of yours?"

"All of that. Everything feels so heavy. I don't have any desire to deal with it."

"That sounds bad, but I get it. It's okay to feel overpowered with stuff. You don't have to be the greatest human on the planet. Just be a regular guy. That's what you're good at."

"The way I've been feeling, I'd love to be a regular guy right now."

"Ethan, you've always been the regular type. And a doofus. But a regular doofus."

"Don't make me laugh."

"Come on. You need to snap out of this. See it for what it is: a temporary storm. Let it go."

"You mean I don't have to believe in time travel?"

"Oh my gosh. Believe in whatever feels right. Science? Santa Claus? Even absurd wishes, if that's what makes you happy."

"I guess I've been stuck in this silly childhood nonsense long enough."

"Finally. You get it. Be a grownup," Gail said.

I could feel another layer of depression peeling away. "Okay, Gail. Grownup-time is here. Thanks."

"No problem, Doofus."

12

Lifted

My storm clouds were breaking apart. I kept Lula's piece of paper and read it often. I thought about all those disappointing Christmases and felt free to celebrate normally—you know—without a vigil. A tinge of the Bona Fide Christmas Expert was re-emerging.

I found Cindy and suggested something that surprised her. "Cindy, let's take a walk."

"Really?"

It was a brilliant fall day as we entered our gorgeous autumn surroundings. "Cindy, I want to apologize for being such a downer. I've turned a corner. I'm excited about the holidays again."

"Hallelujah. I've been worried about my Odd Guy."

"And about the Christmas wish vigil."

"Yes?"

"It's time I had a normal Christmas."

"You mean you'll finally join us for the midnight candlelight service?"

"I'm looking forward to it."

"Promise?"

"I promise. No more waiting for a miracle."

"The kids will be so happy."

My new attitude was fragile, but I could see how it brightened everyone's outlook. And as usual, Cindy couldn't wait to decorate for Christmas. She quickly pulled out all our holiday adornments, and somehow, the Christmas Blanket had become part of her decorating vision.

"Do we really need to see the Christmas Blanket this year?" I asked, still unsure how it would affect me.

"It's not Christmas without the blanket."

As she draped it across Big Chair, it stirred feelings about the wish vigil, but I was okay with seeing it. I told myself it had become just another Christmas decoration.

My fresh eyes could appreciate all that God was doing. I was out of the miry pit. Cindy and I took many walks and were always mesmerized by the Victorian landscape. Our favorite, without a doubt, was the Humphrey's mansion. It displayed lavish filigree and a white picket fence that framed their stately elm tree. Its 1905 charm was a constant reminder of simpler days. But our days leading up to Christmas were far from simple.

With two beautiful kids, it only made sense that dance lessons and play rehearsals would be at the top of our to-do list. Cindy always took the lead in transporting the kids to their respective activities. I became an expert at brushing Shelly's hair and precisely placing her bow. Then, James, having landed the role of lead angel in his school play, required my constant help to learn his lines.

"Okay, James, repeat after me, 'Fear not, for behold, I bring you—"

"I got that part. It's the last part I need help with."

"Okay, listen closely. 'Ye shall find the babe wrapped in swaddling clothes, lying in a manger."

"Ye shall find a ... manger?"

"James, you can do this," I said. "When you're up there on that stage, and it seems scary because everyone is looking at you, let God's peace come to you. It will, and you will feel it. Then you'll become the angel and confidently deliver your lines."

"I sure hope so," he said.

I suspect this run-through will repeat several times right up to curtain time. May he knock it out of the park when he's finally on stage.

�× ✶ ✶

Mingled in with our hectic December, I noticed certain things seemed different. My growing anticipation was made clear when little clues kept popping up, reassuring me that this Christmas would be special. Perhaps because I am no longer a slave to the wish. I can now get on with enjoying the holidays without another disappointing vigil.

About three weeks before Christmas, Dad showed up with a small wooden box. "Here, happy birthday."

I peeked inside and noticed a magnifying glass, a small doily, a little pair of scissors, one angel earring, and Grandma's bifocals. She kept these items next to where she worked on her prize-winning projects.

I lifted her glasses, seeing a finger smudge and a single strand of silver hair lodged in the hinge.

The sight of these sweet treasures kindled a peaceful sadness. It was as though Grandma was telling me, "Ethan, time moves on, and that's okay."

"Well, your mom has more chores for me. I'd better get going."

"Thanks, Dad. I'm so glad you found these. It's the best birthday gift I could ever receive."

Then, about a week later, another clue popped up. It was a substantial package sent from Cousin Gail.

Cindy lugged it from the porch and plopped it on the coffee table. "Let's open it. I'm dying to see what Gail would send us."

I scrutinized the package and told Cindy, "If that's what I think it is, I'm surprised it took Gail so long to send it to us."

"Oh, now I've really got to see what it is," Cindy said, searching for scissors.

"Here, use these," I said, holding Grandma's little scissors.

"Perfect." She opened the package and peered inside. "It seems to be an old—"

"Bible," I finished her sentence.

"Yes. It looks like Grandma's."

I recognized the old family Bible. "Obviously, Gail finally got tired of having it around."

"Well, I've never thought of Gail as a Christian," Cindy said.

Looking at the large Bible, I was excited to see it. I had missed seeing it.

"Oh, look," Cindy said opening Gail's Christmas card. She read,

> *Ethan, Grandma must have been a little out of it when she*
> *gave me this thing. I know she meant for you to have it.*
> *Happy holidays to you all.*
> *–Love, Gail.*

Cindy hoisted the heavy Bible and wobble-walked it to me. "Here, enjoy." Then she quickly disappeared into the Kitchen.

I placed my hands on its cover and reflected on how time changes things. As a child, it never occurred to me that one day I'd be sitting here, a grown man, holding our family Bible and longing for just one more Christmas at Grandma Ada and Papa Nate's little house.

13

A Night of Jubilation

Apparently, I caught Christmas fever as a record number of decorations spread throughout the house. I even filled my shopping cart with Christmas toys and couldn't wait to dive into my notorious wrapping skills. My motto has always been, *Why wrap it normally when you can wrap it weirdly?*

My favorite technique was to add something unexpected. Like the year, I included a sizable candy bar next to the bow on each present. Of course, the kids loved it. And for this particular year, plastic finger rings, blinking with bright LED colors, became our outrageous gift embellishment. I imagined the children's giggles as I attached one ring to each package. And when we tested the blinkers all at once, it was hilarious.

"Your best idea ever," Cindy said.

It surprised me how suddenly Christmas Eve was upon us. Three joyous events would all happen on this one evening. At 6 p.m., James would deliver his well-rehearsed angelic portrayal at his school play. After that, we would rush to Cindy's folks for our family Christmas. The third item was made clear when Cindy said, "Don't forget, we have the midnight candle service with Susie and Jack. You're gonna love it."

It began snowing that evening as we headed to the school for the best

Christmas play ever. The small auditorium had barely enough room for the hordes of families eager to see their darlings on stage. The classic Christmas story would offer plenty of cute mishaps, all to be captured on countless cell phones.

Soon, James made his grand stage appearance. He stood prominently above the scene thanks to a well-secured stepladder hidden behind a cluster of cardboard clouds.

I must have been nervous for Lead Angel James because I caught myself mouthing his every word and beamed with pride, hearing him deliver each line perfectly.

Then the unthinkable happened. In the middle of his stellar proclamation, the power shut off, snapping the room into darkness. Chatter from the audience spread. I pulled out my keychain flashlight and shined it straight at James to ensure he wouldn't tumble off the ladder. But I noticed he was standing perfectly calm. Despite the confusion, he appeared unwilling to relinquish his hard-earned performance. I watched him glance around the room, surveying the rising calamity. He suddenly looked straight ahead and stretched his arms wide. Was he remaining in character? Then, with a resounding command of his angel persona, he continued his lines, loud and clear.

"And this shall be a sign unto you." The crowd quieted as everyone looked at James. "Ye shall find the babe wrapped in swaddling clothes, lying in a manger."

At that perfect instant, the lights clicked back on. The crowd could not contain themselves as they stood applauding for young James. What a moment for everyone in the room to see such courage.

Cindy leaned proudly toward me. "That's our son."

The smiles across the audience showed that they had been significantly uplifted, feeling the joy of Christmas.

As the play ended, Cindy again leaned in, "If you can round up the angel, I'll meet you at the car. I don't want to be late to Mom and Dad's."

Driving to Cindy's parents, I wondered what wackiness her dad, Stan, might have in store.

Christmas Eve dinner at Cindy's folks was always so entertaining. It reminded me of Grandma's house, especially the chaos part. Of course, the food was great, the conversation lively, and the kids supplied joyful chaos.

Cindy reminded me when it was time to hand out presents. We hurriedly turned on each dazzling finger ring so everyone's gift blinkcd brightly as we handed them out. In no time, a colorful light show of rings and smiles paraded all over the room. Even after opening their multitude of presents and with toys scattered everywhere, the flashing rings were still going strong.

When the gift activities had settled down, I noticed Stan quietly digging behind the Christmas tree. He re-emerged, carrying a secret stash of presents that quickly caught everyone's attention. No blinking lights, but we all knew he was up to something.

Once he had everyone's attention, he said, "What do you call it when Santa takes a break?" And before anyone could answer, he said, "A Santa Pause."

His joke sparked a mixture of laughter and groans—well-meaning groans.

"Okay, brace yourselves," he said. "I have a most extraordinary gift for each of you."

"Uh oh," I said, quietly under my breath, but not quietly enough since Cindy delivered a not-so-subtle elbow to my ribs.

Stan sported a ridiculous grin as he handed out his mysterious gifts to all the adults in the room. He had something up his sleeve, but I could not judge since I, myself, had just handed out a bunch of crazy blinking presents.

As the unwrapping began, we quickly realized everyone had all received the same thing, and one by one, we each held up our very own pale yellow flannel bathrobe. Looks of confusion quickly gave way to bursts of laughter, which was obviously the desired effect Stan was hoping for.

Then he insisted, "Everyone put 'em on for an awkward family photo."

It was hilarious to see everyone sporting their lovely new robe. Things got even funnier when Cindy's mom said, "Shall we sing a hymn because we're looking like some kind of crazy choir?"

"I feel like we're all at a spa somewhere," Cindy's sister said.

"More like the Apostles," Cindy added.

There was much laughter that night, with many happy photos and good cheer. Thanks to Stan and myself, this was an extra fun Christmas to remember.

14

From the Mouth of Babes

Snow and slick streets had us arriving home late. Cousin Susie and her husband Jack would soon pick us up for the midnight candlelight service. I sat in Big Chair, reviewing the night's fun photos on my phone, and James walked by, zooming his new toy airplane—his big ring still blinking. "Hey James, great job tonight. You totally became the Angel, didn't you?"

James smiled as he confessed, "I did like you said and asked God to make me strong."

"Yes, he made you super strong. I'm very proud of you."

As James continued playing with his airplane, I leaned back in Big Chair and noticed the little box of Grandma items on my side table. Our tree lights reflected in Grandma's glasses like years before when she read the Christmas story.

I reached over and gently lifted the box. The little doily displayed excellent craftsmanship. And there it was, Grandma's tiny cross peeking from one edge. I knew she had made this as if it were for Jesus.

I imagined how it would be tonight when midnight comes, and I'm not waiting for a wish to happen. Was I ready to let go?

Just then, while I was deep in thought, Shelly danced into the room wearing James' angel costume. It was oversized, with twisted wings and a crooked halo. She stood in front of me, making up a song. "Look at me. I'm an angel. See my wings. I'm an angel." I barely noticed her until she sang louder, "Fear not, I got good tidings."

Those words yanked me out of my thoughts, and I stared intently into her sweet, angelic performance. Suddenly it hit me—Grandma's words: *You'll know you're ready for the wish to come true when you hear the angel's song.*

Wait a minute, what was happening? I was looking directly at a beautiful little angel and hearing her song. Oh my God, was this it? The sign? Am I finally ready?

I lifted Shelly into my arms. "Yes, you are my angel. Grandma Ada told me I would see you someday."

On the verge of tears, I looked up and whispered, "God, I am finally ready. It is your timing, and this little angel says that the time is finally here."

I sat Shelly in Big Chair and raced to our bedroom. "Cindy, I can't go tonight. I have to do the wish vigil."

"Ethan, come on."

"I have to. I now know tonight is the night."

"But you promised."

"I did, and I'm sorry, but tonight it will happen."

Cindy looked down, shaking her head. "I can't believe this. I was so excited you'd finally be with us."

"Just one more Christmas Eve. One more vigil, and I promise that will be the last of it."

Cindy's stern eyes cut into me. "Why now?" she asked.

"Because it's always been about God's timing, not mine. And he's telling me tonight is—"

HONK.

"They're here, kids," Cindy hollered. "Get your coats on. It's time to go."

"I'm so sorry," I said.

Cindy and the kids marched out the door.

"Tell Jack I said to drive—"

SLAM.

The door shut hard with the winter wind. Or was it Cindy's anger?

The room slowly regained its warmth. I took a deep breath and prepared for my last vigil. Everything was there: Christmas tree, mantel clock, Big Chair, and of course, the Christmas Blanket. Other than Cindy's disappointment, everything was in place. With only a few minutes till midnight, I settled into Big Chair and pulled the Christmas Blanket across my lap.

As I had done so many times before, I waited. But this time was different. I felt an assurance that the wish was really about to happen.

Then, I did something never before in my vigil. I began praying. "Dear Lord, I look at this baby blanket so lovingly created by Grandma Ada, and I have a strange sadness. My bittersweet Christmas moments burden me as I long for Grandma and the wish. I know it will take a miracle to travel through time to see your Holy Son, Jesus. It is merely a wish, but just as Grandma would make things and give them to you in her heart, maybe in my heart, I could somehow go back there and experience that special holy night. Please bless this cherished wish and open a small hole in your fabric of time through which I might fully see my Savior's glory as he entered the world. I know all things are possible with you. Father in Heaven, I pray this in the name of Jesus–Amen."

15

Tears of Sorrow, Tears of Joy

I leaned back, pondering the words I had just prayed, and a calmness wrapped around me. I drifted into its peaceful lull and tried to imagine how the wish would unfold.

Gazing at the Christmas tree, I became mesmerized by its soft lights. Then, something strange caught my attention. One bulb shone brighter than the rest. It grew more and more dazzling, defying any sensibility. Was this the beginning of the wish?

Suddenly, the mantel clock chimed. My breathing grew heavy; my eyes locked onto that solitary light as it flared even more radiant.

There, deep in its magnificent glow, I could make out the faint likeness of an angel. I rubbed my eyes in disbelief. Then, looking back, I caught a fleeting vision of a beautiful angelic figure standing by the fireplace. Her radiance filled the room.

But at that instant, there was a jarring commotion outside. The noise startled me, and the angel vanished. What just happened? Did I somehow ruin the wish? Glancing at the clock proved I had been dreaming—it was still seven minutes until midnight.

Again, there was more disturbance at the front door. What was this distraction trouncing on my wish? I opened the door, inspecting the scene for any sign of trouble. But the air was calm, and the gentle snow made everything seem peaceful.

I was about to shut the door when I saw movement on the porch steps. It was a mourning dove, and she seemed distressed. I reached for my jacket, but the only thing within reach was Stan's bathrobe. It would have to do. I added the Christmas Blanket around my shoulders before stepping outside. As I eased my way toward the poor bird, it flailed to the bottom step. "Oh gosh, what can I do to help you?" I needed to get the poor creature out of the cold.

On the porch, I spotted a cardboard box waiting to be used as a bird ambulance. With the box in hand, I approached the dove. She didn't like the box and fluttered further away. I reassured her with my slow, calm voice and readied myself for action.

"Three, two, one." I lunged.

"OUCH!"

If Mrs. Humphrey had been looking out her window, she would have seen a remarkable epic fall. My feet flew one way, and the box flew out of sight. Assessing my failed attempt, I realized I was okay. The bird was still only a few feet away. I couldn't let a little fall keep me from helping the poor creature.

"This is all your fault," I said to the dove.

She tilted her head and seemed amused by my slapstick performance.

I stood and shook the snow from my blanket, prompting my little distraction to hop further away. After a few deep breaths, I resumed my mercy efforts. The dove wanted no part, staying inches out of my reach. My ongoing chase took us some distance along the snow-covered landscape. I finally just stopped and stared at the bird, who was staring back at me. I'm quite sure we looked like two odd figures in a gigantic snow globe.

"Are you my angel?" I heard myself ask. That question surprised me, for it wasn't until that very instant that the thought even crossed my mind. Could this odd little bird actually be my angel? It felt funny to think I might be witnessing the beginnings of a miracle. What if this is how the Christmas wish was coming true?

Right then, the dove turned and flew away. "Wait, don't leave," I said, watching the dove fly into the darkness. I could see there would be no wish coming true out here in the cold. At least the dove was doing better.

"Well, let's see; I am standing here in the snow, wearing a perfectly ridiculous bathrobe and a baby blanket over my head while asking a bird if she's an angel." Realizing the absurdity of my circumstances, I knew it was time to head back.

While Trudging my way home, something caught my eye—a peculiar soft glow on the snow around me. I froze, perfectly still, sensing this was no ordinary light. The glow began to dance with glistening exuberance, and I felt its splendor surrounding me. My body started shaking, for I knew exactly what this was.

I slowly turned, and it was right there—at that moment—I beheld the most incredible sight I had ever seen. I was finally able to look into the dazzling eyes of a magnificent angel. Her hair and flowing gown seemed to dance in a slow, peaceful motion as if synchronized with the rhythm of the universe. There's no way to describe her other than "pure holiness" that radiated around me, filling the air with a scent of divine purity. I could feel her magnificence touching my spirit with comforting warmth. After 42 years of waiting and with so many wish vigils, I uttered only two words, "It's you."

Years of hope were now lifting me into something words cannot describe. I could feel myself entering a blissful state of awe, made even more intense when she spoke. "Yes, Ethan, I am your angel." Her words showered me with even greater warmth, like peaceful sunlight breaking through the clouds on a dark winter's day. "Do not be afraid, for God himself has sent me."

I fell to my knees, looking to Heaven. "Thank you, Father."

I felt unworthy as I peered again at the glorious angel. Her holy features captivated me as she spoke. "Stand, Ethan. Tonight, we journey through time, and you will bear witness to Christ as he enters this world."

"Oh my God," I cried out, my voice trembling with awe and disbelief. "This is real." For the first time, I was experiencing an absolute miracle, the supernatural kind.

"Come," the Angel beckoned, reaching out her hand. "We have far to go and much to see."

I could barely move. Was I dreaming again? It took all my courage, but I stood and followed the Angel. Slow at first, then more assured with each step. I was trying hard to process this indescribable event that was miraculously unfolding before me. Tonight, I would see the infant Jesus.

"Wait! The blanket?" I panicked. Then, reaching, I felt it covering my head. "Yes. Thank you, God."

What was I to make of this journey through time? Walking close behind the Angel, a warm, comforting light cast a soft iridescence on everything around me. I noticed the snowflakes were not falling to the ground, but instead, they seemed to defy gravity, gently rising upwards.

Gradually, my surroundings began to transform before my eyes. Historical scenes unfolded like a living tapestry of the past. The Humphrey's Victorian house stood in its early stages of construction, with their grand elm tree a mere sapling. People from different eras came to life, each living out their own fragment of history. Men adorned in top hats appeared and were swiftly replaced by wooden ships sailing with pilgrims on board. Medieval armies clashed in fierce battles while rustic villagers went about their lives, their donkey carts ambling by so close I could have reached out and touched them.

Absorbing each unveiled encounter, I was afraid to blink. I didn't want to miss even a second of this glorious miracle that carried me deeper into history toward the Nativity. I was filled with pure delight.

As we continued our journey, gratitude welled up within me, and I found myself whispering thanks to God with every step. My anticipation of what lay ahead felt exhilarating. It was like a perfect song, harmonizing with the joy in my heart. I marveled at how it could possibly get any better.

But then, unexpectedly, a strange darkness descended upon me, shattering the beauty of the moment. It was a sensation that did not fit with my beautiful miracle wish. I fell to my knees with overwhelming sorrow and buried my head in my hands. What was this? I was crying, and through my sobbing, the Angel could hear me exclaim, "I didn't realize this would be part of the journey."

I felt the Angel's touch as she spoke kindly to my spirit, "Ethan, time cannot conceal the truth. We must pass this way to reach our destination."

"I know, but I can't do this."

"Tonight, you are a witness to your Lord Jesus."

"But why this?"

I buried my eyes hard into my hands, my mind in turmoil. Then, after a moment, I slowly raised my head, looking at the lifeless body of Jesus Christ, the Son of God, nailed to a cross. My voice choked with tears as I said, "This was not supposed to be part of the wish. Grandma never mentioned it."

The Angel had become quiet, and when I looked at her face, I could see her tears glistening in the dim light. Then, the Angel turned to me and said, "Rejoice, Ethan, for what you are witnessing right now is pure love. This was his wish. His wish for your redemption."

I knew she was right, but all I could do was kneel beneath the cross, staring at the blood-stained ground and trying to bear this moment.

Then, I heard my Angel say, "Tonight, God is giving you a gift. He loves you very much, and someday you will realize how great a gift you are now receiving."

With my head bowed, I mourned in silence. And after a moment, the Angel's form suddenly glowed brighter. "Behold, Ethan," she declared. "Your wish lies just ahead."

I looked up, straining to see through my tears. Then I saw it. There was no longer any doubt that this was my wish, and now, it was in full view right in front of me. I could see with my own eyes the little town of Bethlehem.

Gripping The Christmas Blanket, I cried, "Father God, you did it. I am here. The wish is real." My tears were now tears of joy. I wiped them with the blanket trying to see more clearly the beloved town still far away There was no mistaking its distinctive features It was all there: the soft glow of torch lights glimmering among the buildings, the trees, the travelers entering the gates This was better than any Christmas card could ever depict. It was the real thing.

I again felt my Angel's gentle touch as she beckoned, "Come, Ethan, for the hour draws near."

"Yes, of course," I answered.

As I stood, adjusting my blanket, the Angel said, "Please tell me about this covering."

"Oh, my Christmas Blanket? It is a gift made especially for Jesus. I have been its caretaker my whole life, and tonight, I will give it to its rightful owner."

"It is beautiful and a worthy gift for a king," she replied.

She then smiled, pointing to Bethlehem. My heart was bursting with anticipation, and without thought, I began to run toward the breathtaking sight. I was running through the Holy Land—a tricky endeavor while wearing house slippers. But I was not hindered as I focused on the wondrous destination ahead.

I ran with all my strength, feeling the supernatural allure of my miracle wish. I ran, lifting the blanket high to the sky, gleefully challenging my Angel to a race. She smiled. I kept running and trying to imagine what it would be like to finally see the Nativity—the actual Nativity.

It felt strange to be miles away and centuries away from everything I've ever known. But somehow, with the Christmas Blanket with me, it all seemed right. Though every law of nature and physics had been broken, God's touch was upon me, making all this what it should be.

.

16

Fear Not

There I was, living my wish at full speed when something again seemed wrong. I stopped to catch my breath and looked down. "What's happening?" I shouted. My feet were not touching the ground. I looked at my Angel and could see we were rising in midair. Panic was taking over, and then I noticed her gentle expression. She was again reassuring me that everything was as it should be. I welcomed her calming demeanor, but still, I was confused. Why were we not speeding along to the wish? What was this odd interruption?

The Angel answered my thoughts with perfect softness. "Ethan, we are lifted up by God himself. Let us feel the joy of this night. It's the joy that all of Heaven is feeling, and we must share it with the world."

I turned and gazed across miles of Holy Land, feeling so much joy. That's when I saw them. "Of course," I said. "It's the shepherds. They are tending their flocks."

Before I could dwell on this breathtaking sight, I quickly realized that my Angel and I had become *their* breathtaking sight. They were terrified to see us.

The Angel was looking at me. Her head tilted as she said, "This is *your* moment."

Oh my God, this was not part of the wish. The Angel nudged me and gestured toward the excited shepherds. I knew what I was being asked to do. Then I remembered I knew the lines. I knew every word. All that rehearsing, I thought it was for young James, but it wasn't. It was for me.

Each second I hesitated, the shepherds became more alarmed until finally, I proclaimed, "Fear not."

Oh no, what just happened? Is this for real? Am I actually speaking here? Have I become part of the Bible?

The Angel smiled, and I knew it was my time, my wish. The shepherd's eyes were fixed on me. I looked to Heaven, asking, "Father, give me strength."

Then I continued, "For, behold, I bring you good tidings of great joy, which shall be to all people. For unto you is born this day in the city of David, a Savior, which is Christ the Lord."

Right then, I turned to the Angel, about to ask if they could understand what I was saying, but I noticed she had become beautifully luminescent, way beyond her usual glow. Then, to my astonishment, I, too, was glowing with the same heavenly light. No! No way am I worthy of this. How could God allow it? Me, part of the Heavenly Host? My mind was struggling, and my spirit was soaring as I again felt encouragement from the Angel. I looked at the shepherds and delivered the last line with peace and confidence. "And this shall be a sign unto you; Ye shall find the babe wrapped in swaddling clothes, lying in a manger."

Oh God, I did it. I drew a deep breath, thinking of James and how proud he'd be of his dad. And like courageous James, I became the Angel.

But this was only the beginning. I heard beautiful singing. The melodic tones were unlike any I have ever heard. No human voice could ever achieve such glorious notes. It was far beyond anything imaginable. If the most beautiful soft breeze drifted through the most beautiful forest, its tender resonance would pale compared to what my heart was hearing.

I turned and beheld a million angels, filling the heavens with unbelievable harmony. And me in their midst. There are simply no words in human language to describe how magnificent that moment was for everyone, especially me.

The glory of Heaven was so bright and mighty that I could actually feel God's presence and the joy that he, himself, must be feeling. His words, *on Earth, as it is in Heaven,* rang through me, touching my spirit. I wanted this part of my wish to never end. I knew it would soon fade back into its usual starlit darkness. But for that moment, I rested in the heart of Heaven. I smiled because I knew Jesus had now arrived.

I was soon back on the ground, trying to sort through this night's astonishing holy affairs. It was so much more than I could have ever imagined. Still in a daze, I gazed at Bethlehem's golden aura shining against the deep sky. The sight tugged at me.

I told the Angel, "Just think, my Lord and Savior is right there, born this very night." But the Angel did not answer. She was gone. Oh no. Did she fade into the night sky along with the Heavenly Host? Was I now on my own? I looked back at the little town that beckoned me from its hilltop perch. My Lord was lying there within those walls. What was I waiting for?

"No more delay," I shouted as I again set out toward my wish and my Savior. I ran and pushed myself hard, as only a Bona Fide Christmas Expert would do when running straight into the very first Noel. The beautiful scene loomed brighter with each stride.

Finally, reaching Bethlehem's main gate, I collapsed. I didn't realize how exhausted I had become. This middle-aged body was not happy. Resting on my knees and trying to catch my breath, I realized how pathetic I must look to those passing by.

After resting for a moment and about to resume my journey, I saw a man of elegant appearance on a camel coming near. He was breathtaking, and I realized this was no ordinary pilgrim. I studied him closely, discerning the graceful floral pattern glistening across his robe. Then, as he came closer, torchlight revealed the full dramatic splendor of this desert traveler.

Not far behind came two more amazing camel-back travelers. One of them smiled with compassion as he looked at me. Could he see my awestruck expression? He then tossed me a coin. It was a lustrous little piece of gold. I rose to my feet, gesturing my thanks for his kindness.

The three strolled by, along with their entourage, and I could see the excitement on their faces. Their long journey's mission was about to be fulfilled, and I felt a surprising kinship with these ancient seekers. If I could only tell them that I, too, have traveled a long distance to worship the Holy Son of God.

My heart was whirling with all that surrounded me: Bethlehem's glowing entrance, the soothing night breeze, and the sight of majestic travelers. It was a scene made so much better because it was real, and I was part of it. Time had been handed to me, and I held that moment tight. Even though I was standing 2,000 years in the past, I knew this was *my time.*

I could feel God's own joy whirling around me as if to say that my wish was his wish, too.

✶ ✶ ✶

Basking in God's glorious respite, I knew it was time to resume my journey. Pulling the Christmas Blanket tightly over my head, I suddenly realized that my appearance blended in quite well with those around me. I was wearing my flannel robe, slippers that looked somewhat like sandals, and my Christmas blanket hooded over my head. I indeed felt like a Bible character, and for a tiny instant in time, I guess that is what God was allowing me to become.

Entering the gate proved Bethlehem was a busy place, not at all lying still, as the classic Christmas carol suggests. The narrow streets were bustling with people and animals traveling in all directions

Where to look? Where should I go? Then, I spotted a stable, partially hidden by a wall. Could this be the one—the birthplace of a savior?

I began walking, dodging through hundreds of people, and focused on the site ahead. I suddenly felt the Christmas Blanket fall from my head. I turned and saw a disheveled woman clutching the blanket. She flashed a disturbed expression before swiftly making her getaway.

I was not about to let anyone take this cherished gift from me. I tore through the crowd, gaining on the thief. She was fast and knew her way around, but I was determined, darting with surprising middle-aged agility. Finally, I maneuvered close, and then, with all my strength, I lunged, grabbing one end of the blanket. She glared straight at me. Her grip was determined, but so was mine. Our eyes locked, neither of us blinking. I studied her red eyes. Her youthful face was weathered and stained with sad tears.

As I noticed her pained features, a strange thing happened. It was something that betrayed all common sense. I let go. I simply released my grip. The woman and blanket vanished into the night.

What had just happened? This was my prized blanket, the one possession I'd had my entire life. It was the gift meant for Jesus. And now, in a split second, it was gone. Was Satan trying to spoil my wish?

All I could do was stand in the middle of Bethlehem, feeling the weight of this terrible loss. I was grieving. If only I had held it tighter. It seemed I had turned my back on the blanket and everything it represents: love, joy, and its connection to this beautiful, holy night.

Amid my despair, I heard a small voice from inside. "It's all right," the voice said. "You peered into the woman's eyes, saw the hurt, and could feel her anguish. So, you gave. The part of you that knows God's heart was willing to give. You released something extremely dear to you, exactly like God himself is doing on this very night, and so it is all right."

I lifted my eyes, and there in front of me was my Angel. Of course, I knew those were her words. She had again been speaking encouragement into my spirit. She smiled, reaching out her hand.

Walking toward my Angel, I stopped, halted by her appearance. Maybe it was the lighting or the way she stood, but right then, she looked exactly like the Angel on the Christmas Blanket. The shape of her gown and her outstretched arm suddenly seemed so familiar and comforting.

The crowd had dwindled. The Angel tenderly took my hand and guided me along the stone street into the final steps of my wish. I peered anxiously in every direction, searching for the scene I knew only as a tranquil rendering.

Our walk reminded me of our earlier time travel cadence. But this was no longer about time; it was about my Lord Jesus. Oh, what a night, with so many tears of joy, and I knew God had much more to come. That's why I was not surprised when the light around me grew brighter and golden.

The Angel and I gazed upward. "The Star," I shouted. "It's his Star!" The sparkling brightness was so beautiful, and I wondered why I had not noticed it sooner? I've seen it so often portrayed in paintings and movies that encountering the real Star now was like finding an old friend.

I felt my Angel's arm around my shoulder, guiding me. I wondered if my heart could bear any more. Walking there alongside one of God's beautiful angels brought overwhelming joy. But something beyond joy was rising inside me. I was shaking with exhilaration. I couldn't help but stop and lift my hands to Heaven and spin in joyous circles right there in the starlight. This was so out of character for me, but I couldn't stop myself. My Angel felt it, too, for she also was turning in circles with lifted hands. Without a doubt, we were praising God in the most beautiful way possible.

After our impromptu praise, I rested, absorbing the peaceful starlight. That's when something caught my eye. I saw a scene.—it was *the* scene. My emotions overflowed as I gazed at the most beautiful Nativity image. No one had to tell me; I knew this was the place, and I was trembling.

The Angel and I proceeded, savoring each step toward this miracle. How many Christmas carols have been written about this very night? The Star's glow encircled the entire scene with holy light. Each step brought me closer to the manger and my wish. I saw Joseph standing with Mary as shepherds knelt close by. Each step closer filled me with more holy delight.

I'm here, in this place and time. It is not just a glimpse—God has lifted me up to see. I kept thinking, "If only Gail or everyone else could see this, they would understand." They would know God's love and would believe.

Finally, reaching the stable, I could barely breathe. I felt so unworthy to be in the presence of God himself. But there I was, just a few steps from my Lord, the world's Savior.

My heart seemed much too small to take in all the miraculous glory surrounding me. Then Joseph smiled at me with tiredness in his eyes and spoke one word, "Come."

I was captivated by the tiny manger, where each careful step revealed more and more of the baby's face. Finally, I was next to him, the light of the world.

The wish was happening right in front of me right now. All I could think was to drop to my knees and bow my head. I could hear myself whispering. "Father in Heaven, you did it. The wish is real, and it's happening right now. You have blessed me with so much more than a wish. I'm sorry I have no gift for you."

Kneeling next to the manger, I was amazed by how the Star's holy light made everything appear even more beautiful.

Then, I heard a voice. A familiar voice behind me said, "Oh, it's just as I imagined it would be."

I turned to see Grandma Ada smiling at me. She looked young and radiant. Her eyes sparkled with tears. My own tears began streaming down my cheeks as she embraced me. How much could my heart take in one night? Of course, Grandma Ada would be here. That was our plan. The wish began with her.

As Grandma Ada and I knelt, our hearts filled with the wonder of this miraculous moment. I watched Grandma, knowing what she would do. She extended her hand and tenderly touched the face of the Baby Jesus. Overwhelmed with joy, she met the gaze of the holy infant, his eyes reflecting the starlight. Mary could see the love that Grandma Ada and I felt for her son. Despite her weariness, Mary rose to her knees and took Grandma's hands, finding solace in a mother's touch.

Just then, Jesus made a breathy sound of contentment, and Mary wrapped his little face in her hands.

Surrounded by splendor and glory, Grandma slowly turned and gave me a look. It was her serious look. "Ethan. Have you forgotten something?"

"Oh, Grandma, I'm so—"

"This, perhaps," she said, reaching under her wrap and revealing the Christmas Blanket.

"What? Where did you find it?" But before she could answer, I heard myself say, "Wait, I don't need to know. On this night of miracles, God would never allow the wish to happen without the Christmas Blanket."

It didn't matter how the blanket found its way to Grandma. The important thing is that the Christmas Blanket was now with us. We placed our hands together on the beloved creation. I looked one last time upon the images that had blessed me my whole life. The stars, the trees, the doves, and the special angel were all ready to fulfill their real purpose.

My voice felt weak and cracked as I spoke, "Goodbye, Christmas Blanket. It's time to fulfill your destiny."

We extended the little quilt toward Mary. Her face beamed with genuine delight as she unfolded our offering. She seemed moved by each of its vivid depictions. Then, with loving care, she gently spread it over the infant's tiny body.

I gazed at the Christmas Blanket draped over Jesus and noticed how glorious it appeared, resting in its rightful place. I had beheld this work of art thousands of times and in many settings, but it never looked as beautiful as now.

I finally realized that this was the real purpose of the blanket. It had always been with me, pointing to the wish, driving me toward this moment. God blessed Grandma and me this night in a manner that far exceeded our highest hopes.

The Christ Child looked at the two of us. His eyes were so peaceful, and his face so precious. This sight captured our hearts.

But God was not finished with the wish. Mary smiled, looking straight at Grandma. Then she lifted the holy infant, wrapped in swaddling clothes, and added the Christmas Blanket around him. Grandma shook her head in disbelief as Mary handed her the Christ Child.

Oh, my God, we never imagined the wish could be filled with such elation. Grandma tenderly took her Savior and held him close, feeling His tiny body alive in her arms. His soft baby's breath must have felt warm against her cheek. Tears ran down her face as she repeated, "Thank you, God, thank you,

God," After a peace-filled moment, she returned the holy infant Jesus to Mary. Grandma sighed as she turned to me with an expression that was way beyond pure joy. I'm sure my countenance mirrored what she was feeling.

"Ethan, here we are. Look around; we're in the wish.

"I know. It feels strange," I said. "After so many years of expecting and the empty vigils, God finally found us to be ready."

"Yes. It was God's timing—his perfect timing."

I gazed into Grandma's eyes and knew the Angel would soon carry us back home, but something welled up from deep inside. My voice was weak as I began singing *Silent Night,* and Grandma joined in. I'm sure we were a curious sight, and our singing was not so pretty. But for Grandma and me at the actual Nativity, it was the most beautiful rendition we had ever heard. We absorbed the wonder of our blessed wish as we looked into each other's faces. After one verse, we paused to relish these last moments together.

"Grandma, this song will not be written for another 1800 years."

Grandma smiled at the thought, then added, "Tonight, this beautiful song is made timeless."

I took her hands and said, "Thank you, Grandma, for the wish—for all of this glorious night."

She smiled and said, "Ethan, this would not have been my wish if it didn't include you."

�とし
 ✌ ✌ ✌

The wish was now complete. Time had done its job. As Grandma and I rose to our feet, we hugged. I had missed her so much. So, we just rested in each other's arms. We could tell that something was happening even as we held each other. The Angel was returning us to our own time.

Grandma whispered, "Ethan, our wish is no longer a wish, is it?"

"You're right, Grandma; the wish is now fulfilled."

I thought it strange that the wish was fulfilled centuries before it was ever wished. God is so wonderful.

Later, I would come to realize that the wish that belonged to Grandma Ada and me was never really a wish at all. It was a prayer. And on this one miraculous night, our prayer was answered.

17

My Burning Eyes

What can be said concerning our return to the present time? It was not a dream. I knew it was the loving hand of God, and it was God who had brought the wish into reality. But all I remember about returning to my time was a sudden gust of cold air and finding myself back in my snow-covered front yard with Grandma Ada still holding me tight.

Grandma had concern in her voice. "Are you okay, Ethan? Are you okay?"

"I'm okay. I'm fine."

I leaned back to see her face and reassure her, but when I looked into her eyes, it was not Grandma. It was Cindy. I shook my head and rubbed my eyes. Then, looking around, I could see Cindy and the kids, along with Susie and Jack, standing close by. Jack was dialing for help on his cell phone.

"Wait," I cried out. "Please don't call anyone."

Cindy studied my teary face, which reflected the emotional experience I had just gone through. "Let's get you inside where it's warm," she said, her voice filled with concern.

With everyone inside, Cindy began her interrogation. "Look at you in your robe, roaming around outside. You must have been freezing."

I was still trying to process the night's events. My eyes were burning from the cold wind, or more likely from the many tears I had poured out on this night. I was desperate to tell everyone about all the fantastic things I had just experienced, but where to start?

I could see everyone's concern, so I anxiously began sharing my miracle. "Something happened tonight, something wonderful. Cindy, the wish came true. A miracle has happened." I disregarded Cindy's leery expression and continued. "Now, I know this is going to sound pretty weird, but just moments ago, I was standing in the streets of Bethlehem 2,000 years in the past."

"I'm calling 911," Jack declared as he again dug out his cell phone.

"No, Jack. I'm fine, really. You've all heard me talk about Grandma Ada and our wish."

"Yes, everyone has heard about the outrageous wish," Cindy spouted.

James said, "I remember you told me that story, Daddy."

"Yes, I did, James, and guess what? Tonight, it came true. I saw Grandma Ada. She was there with me. The shepherds, Mary and Joseph, they were all there." I looked upward and continued my story. "The star was shining bright from Heaven, just like it says in the Bible. Then I saw him, the Infant Jesus. So beautiful he was. His eyes were radiant with holy light. You can't describe holy light; you just have to see it. Grandma and I were filled with unimaginable joy as we gave the blanket to Mary. The Christmas baby blanket, entrusted to me as its keeper for so many years, has finally made it to its godly place."

Cindy looked away and seemed distressed by what I was saying. But with the excitement in my voice, surely she could see that something extraordinary had happened tonight.

I knew all this sounded insane, but I kept talking, "Look, I was really there, and I can tell you every detail about Bethlehem, the manger, the streets, everything. Just ask me anything about this night."

Jack asked, "Did the baby have a halo? You see it in paintings."

"There was no halo, but his eyes—I can't explain—it's like they had the appearance of Heaven's glory."

"Was the manger a cave?"

"It was a cave, but a wooden structure was added over its entrance. It was perfect and beautiful. The instant I saw it, I knew it was the Nativity.

My audience, especially Cindy, still seemed skeptical, but I continued, "The whole town was unbelievable, and it felt strange knowing it was the real place and time. In the gentle breeze, I could hear people and livestock.

"Did you see their donkey?" James asked.

"Yes. A sleepy little donkey lay curled up in the back of the stable. He was gray and very fuzzy. I'm sure he belonged to Mary and Joseph."

"Was the star pretty?" Shelly asked.

"Sweetheart, you would not believe how that golden star glimmered and sparkled so brightly."

Shaking her head, Cindy said, "Okay, we'll talk more about this later. Let's get you into bed. We all need some sleep."

"Yes, I'll check in with you tomorrow," Susie said.

I was exhausted as I lay down, but with so many vivid scenes dancing through my spirit, I could not sleep. I got up, found Big Chair, and in my heart, I replayed my night of miracles. Seeing the actual Nativity and the Christ child instilled me with God's love. I did not want this feeling to end.

It was then I heard my Angel speak once more. I could not see her, but I knew her voice. "Ethan, your wish did not happen in just one night. It has been happening your whole life. And now the wish continues as a mission. You are an eyewitness to the birth of Jesus. Many of your generation have lost the true meaning of Christmas. But you were there. You know it is not a fairy tale. Your firsthand account is a gift that can renew the hearts and minds of people today."

I listened to the Angel's peaceful words and felt comforted. I knew this glorious night would never fade from my heart, for my Father will always lift me up to feel and remember the first Noel.

With my wish still glowing in my heart, I soon drifted into a tranquil sleep, and the morning sun awakened me to a new beginning. I was now a changed man whose impossible wish had become a miracle blessing.

18

You're Crazy

Cindy avoided any mention of my miraculous night. The wish should have been a joyous event worth sharing with the world. But a shadowy spirit had settled over our home in the form of Cindy's skepticism. She was quiet. I tried to read her thoughts on the matter. She seemed unable to accept any of it and upset that I would make up, let alone believe in such an outlandish tale. I hated she was questioning my honesty.

I finally had to come right out and ask her, "I can see you're troubled. What is going through your head?"

She crashed down in Big Chair, hurling a skeptical look. "I'll be honest. I'm afraid you're crazy. You must have banged your head that night, and somehow you dreamed something. I mean, you've talked about the wish for years now. You've thought about it so much, so of course, you know every detail, and you believe it ... But I—" She sighed and looked away.

"Cindy, it's true. Please believe me."

"You asked, and I told you. That's what's going through my head. That's all I can offer."

I leaned closer and said, "I know how it sounds, but God is big. Big enough to do mighty miracles. He waited until I was ready. He chose the perfect time to send me back there."

"And why would God do such a thing?"

"Because God is good and loving. Cindy, please don't miss seeing the miracle."

She looked away. "I want to believe you. I can see that you—"

"THE COIN!" I shouted, jumping to my feet.

"What?"

"Remember? I told you about the man on the camel at the gate. He tossed me a coin."

I ran to the bedroom, checking through my robe. "Oh, please let it be here." Cindy entered, watching me franticly dig. "It's not here," I said. "I'm certain I put right here."

I went to the closet, searching the floor, while Cindy checked the dresser.

I frenzied through every inch, finding nothing.

"Ethan, you said it was little and shiny?"

I looked up. Cindy was holding a small piece of gold. A huge smile crept across my face. Our eyes widened, and Cindy jumped into my arms.

"That's it!" I hollered. "It must have fallen into the drawer. Now, do you believe me?"

Cindy broke from our embrace, and her excitement turned serious. "You know, you could have bought this coin," she said.

I paused, then said, "Really? Would Mr. Tightwad spend that kind of money just to fool everyone? And why would I wait three days to spring it on you?"

Cindy studied the golden evidence. "Well, it's not like anything I've ever seen."

I reached for Cindy's arms, gently pulling her close. Then, whispering in her ear, I said, "Cindy, I was there ... I was really there."

She embraced me tighter, and with tears in her voice, she replied, "I know ... I believe."

After a moment, Cindy pulled away, saying, "Do you remember that night at your apartment when you first told me about your wish. And how it troubled me that you totally believed in it?"

"Yes, I was heartbroken when you left."

"I was too," she said, "I had two dreadful days trying to understand your crazy wish. Then, God did something remarkable. He showed me the bookmark on my nightstand. I could see one giant word: *HOPE.* And below was a verse from Psalm 31:24, which read, *Be strong and take heart, all you who HOPE in the Lord.* It suddenly hit me. God was showing me that your *wish* to see Jesus was actually your *hope* in the Lord." She hugged me again and said, "Ethan, I'm sorry for doubting your wish—your hope."

In the following days, the gloom of Cindy's disbelief had vanished, and our lives became more agreeable. It felt good to be back in her trust.

Lately, I've spent much time in Big Chair, reflecting on the many blessings surrounding the wish. I've found it surprising how Christmas carols now mean so much more. Whenever I hear *Joy to The World* or any of the beloved songs that mention that night, I am filled with unspeakable joy. After all, I was there. Every detail comes flying back to my mind.

Today, I discovered another blessing when Grandma's enormous family Bible called to me. I heaved the book to my lap, wondering how Grandma could handle such a weighty volume. The embossed cover lured my fingers across its pebbly surface, and as expected, I could feel Grandma's presence. I opened it where my bookmark had rested for many years and was delighted to find it still marked The Blessed Rs. Then I realized I could finally learn the riddle behind Grandma Ada's mysterious cutoff of the Blessed Rs.

I quickly hid the passages with my hand and uncovered them one by one. Reading them aloud, I could hear Grandma's voice. I finally came to the verse that always halted her: *Blessed are the pure in heart.*

Then I paused. This was becoming an intriguing mystery. I was finally about to learn Grandma's secret passage. Slowly, I lifted my hand and noticed that Grandma had underlined the second part of the scripture. I read, *for they will see God.*

I closed the Bible and leaned back, chuckling. "Good one, Grandma."

She must have known I would someday discover her subtle secret message that pointed squarely at the wish. It was what she hadn't recited all those years ago that now echoed through my soul. Perhaps she knew back then that with pure hearts, we would actually see God.

I continued reflecting on my many years of wishing: the miracle night of time travel, the sight of Baby Jesus lying in the manger, and the one small thing that lovingly wrapped everything together—the Christmas Blanket.

Epilogue

So much has happened in my life, centered on the Christmas Blanket and the Wish. With the wish now fulfilled and the blanket in its proper place, I have a wonderful sense of completion. No more need for a wish vigil. No more anticipation of an angel's visit. And surprisingly, I do not miss these. Well, maybe just a little, but I am very content knowing God chose me for a small part of his plan for humankind.

Some claim that the age of miracles ended with the apostles, but I can say, with blessed assurance, that miracles can still happen.

There is one other thing—something Cindy and I never saw coming. It might be the most notable occurrence of this entire story, one that I am still trying to comprehend.

Arriving home from work one evening, Cindy greeted me with a curious discovery. Holding my time travel bathrobe, she asked me in a serious tone if I had hurt myself on the night of my wish.

"No," I answered, "my fall on the front lawn was nothing."

"Then what is this?" She was holding up the robe and pointing to drops of dried blood.

We looked at each other, then back at the stains. I squinted my eyes, and my mind raced for an answer. Then, a profound thought hit me—the crucifixion.

"Oh my God, Cindy, I was there. Could this be the blood of Jesus? Are we looking at the actual shed blood of the Lamb of God?"

Shaking her head in confusion, Cindy looked up to Heaven and asked, "God, is this for real?"

I took the robe, put it on like the night of my wish, and dropped to my knees. Cindy and I could see the bloodstains were precisely where you would expect if someone had knelt beneath the actual cross of Jesus Christ.

I closed my eyes, replaying the moment. My time at the cross was short as the Angel urged me toward Bethlehem. But I vividly remember dripping blood covering the ground directly below Jesus.

"Cindy, the cross experience was so emotional for me. It was dark, and my eyes were filled with tears, so I couldn't say with certainty if I saw any blood drip onto my clothing. But now, thinking back, I'm not so sure I could have avoided it."

"Oh my God, no one will ever believe this is really the blood of Christ, but what else could it be?" Cindy said.

I put my arm around her as we stared at this overwhelming discovery. All I could say was, "We need to pray and trust that God has something in mind for this and us."

It's been some time since our troubling, beautiful discovery. Anyone passing by our house would never dream that inside, hidden in a small cardboard box, tucked away on the top shelf of a hall closet, one could find a slightly worn bathrobe marked with the actual shed blood of Jesus Christ.

Cindy and I rarely talked about this silent treasure in our possession, but we were both aware of its extreme importance. We sensed God had something significant in store for us. But for now, all we can do is wait upon the Lord.

"... but those who HOPE in the Lord
will renew their strength.
They will soar on wings like eagles;
they will run and not grow weary,
they will walk and not be faint."

–Isaiah 40:31 (NIV)

Phillip W. Cooper is an imaginative story-teller passionate about crafting outlandish tales that warm the heart. His debut novella, "The Christmas Blanket," is a perfect example of his two favorite themes: hope and God's love.

Phillip is a University of Tulsa Art School graduate and a Fellowship of Christian Writers member. He and his wife, Fonda, live in Tulsa, Oklahoma, where they enjoy their family, friends, and two dogs.

Made in United States
North Haven, CT
29 December 2024

63670990R00090